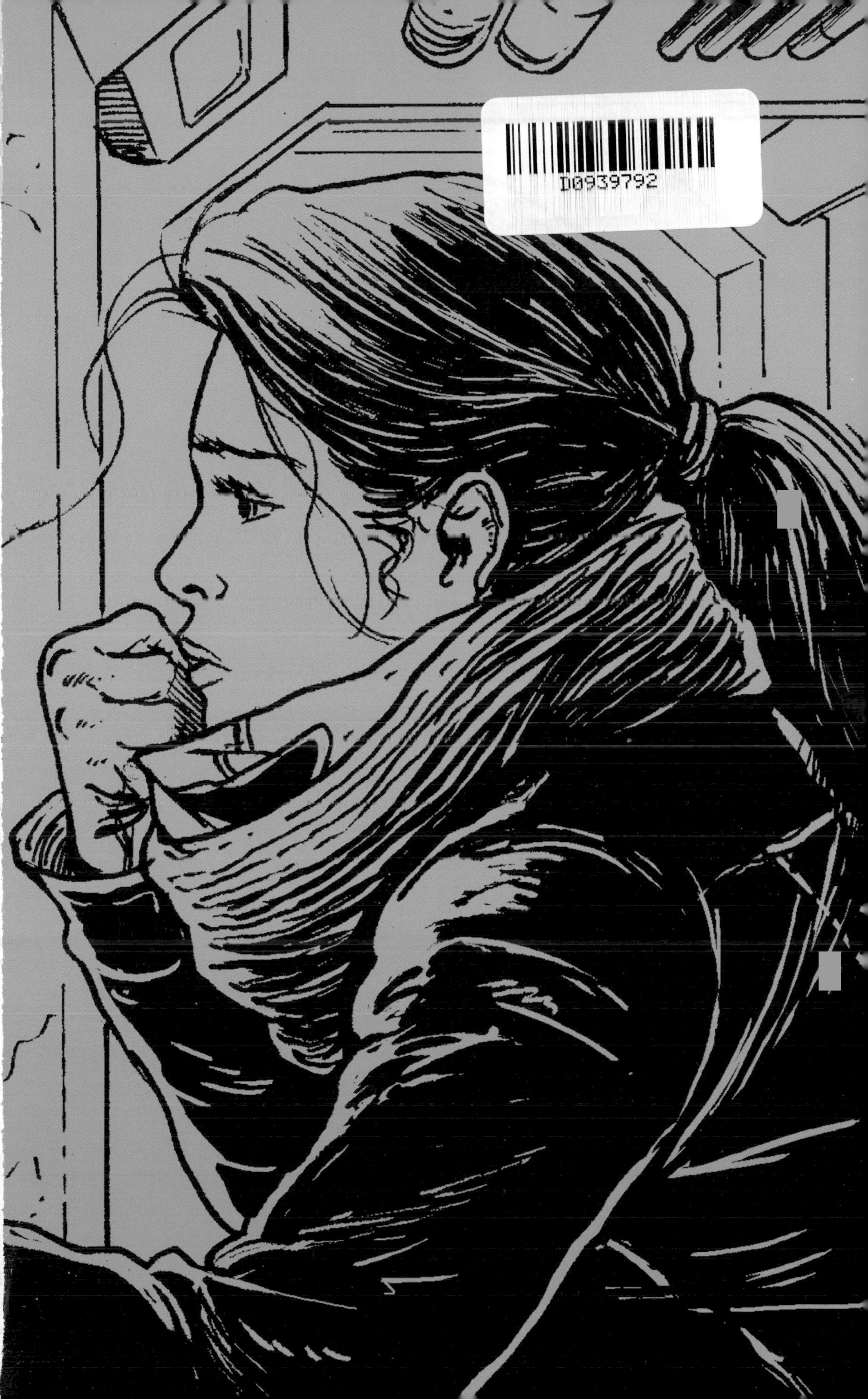

Canada Council for the Arts | Conseil des arts du Canada

We acknowledge the support of the Canada Council for the Arts
Nous remercions le Conseil des arts du Canada de son soutien.

HighWater Press gratefully acknowledges the financial support of the Province of Manitoba through the Department of Sport, Culture and Heritage and the Manitoba Book Publishing Tax Credit, and the Government of Canada through the Canada Book Fund (CBF), for our publishing activities.

HighWater Press is an imprint of Portage & Main Press.
Printed and bound in Canada by Friesens
Design by Jennifer Lum
Cover Art by Scott B. Henderson
Colouring by Donovan Yaciuk
Lettering by Andrew Thomas

Library and Archives Canada Cataloguing in Publication
Title: Version control / David A. Robertson ; Scott B. Henderson ; Donovan Yaciuk.
Names: Robertson, David, 1977- author. | Henderson, Scott B., artist. | Yaciuk, Donovan, 1975- artist.
Description: Series statement: The Reckoner rises ; 2
Identifiers: Canadiana (print) 20210246782 | Canadiana (ebook) 20210246944 | ISBN 9781553799672 (softcover) | ISBN 9781553799689 (EPUB) | ISBN 9781553799696 (PDF)
Subjects: LCGFT: Fantasy comics. | LCGFT: Graphic novels.
Classification: LCC PN6733.R63 V47 2022 | DDC j741.5/971—dc23

25 24 23 22 1 2 3 4 5

MIX
Paper from responsible sources
FSC® C016245
FSC www.fsc.org

HIGHWATER PRESS

www.highwaterpress.com
Winnipeg, Manitoba
Treaty 1 Territory and homeland of the Métis Nation

THE RECKONER RISES

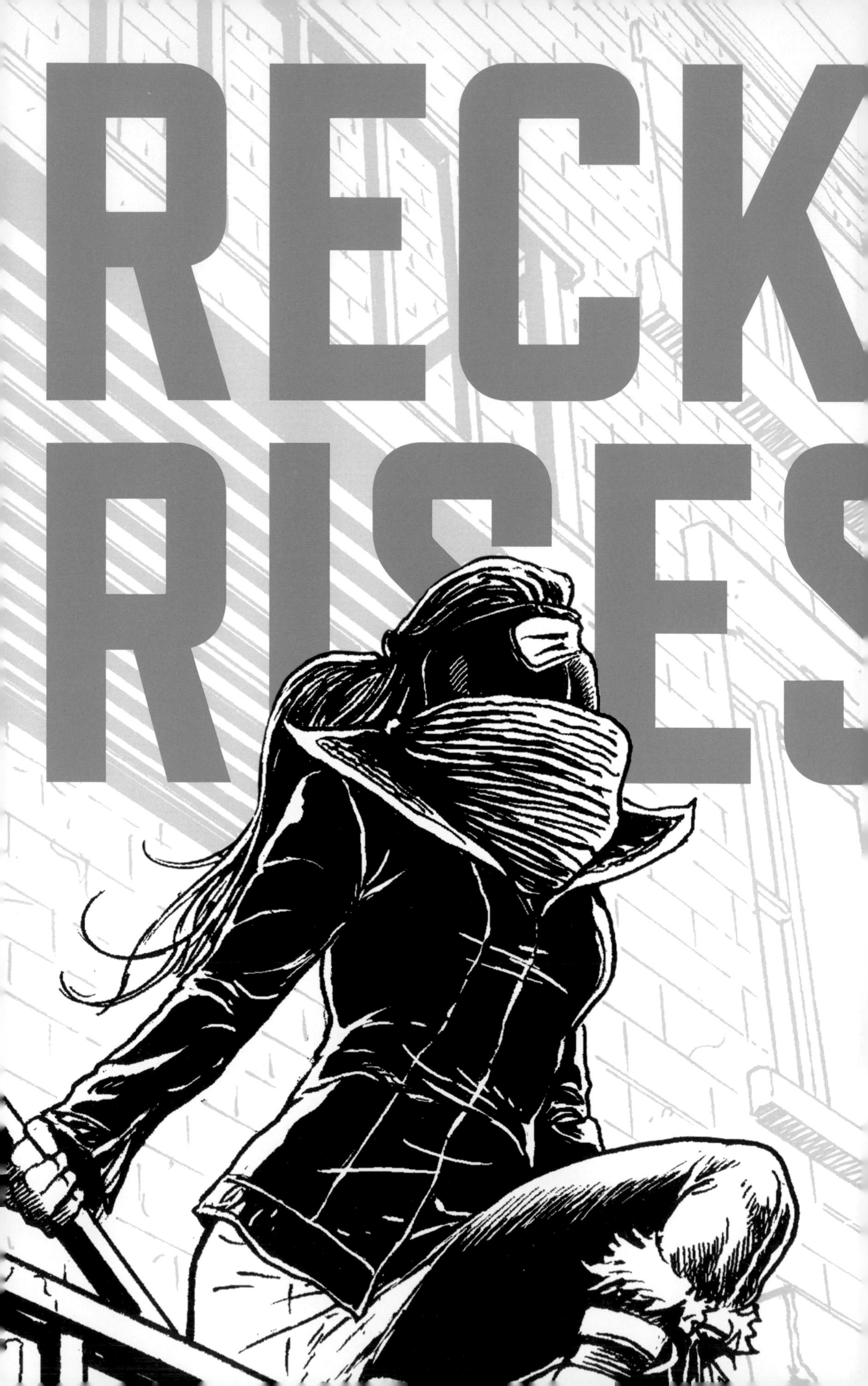
RECK
RISES

ONER

VOLUME 2

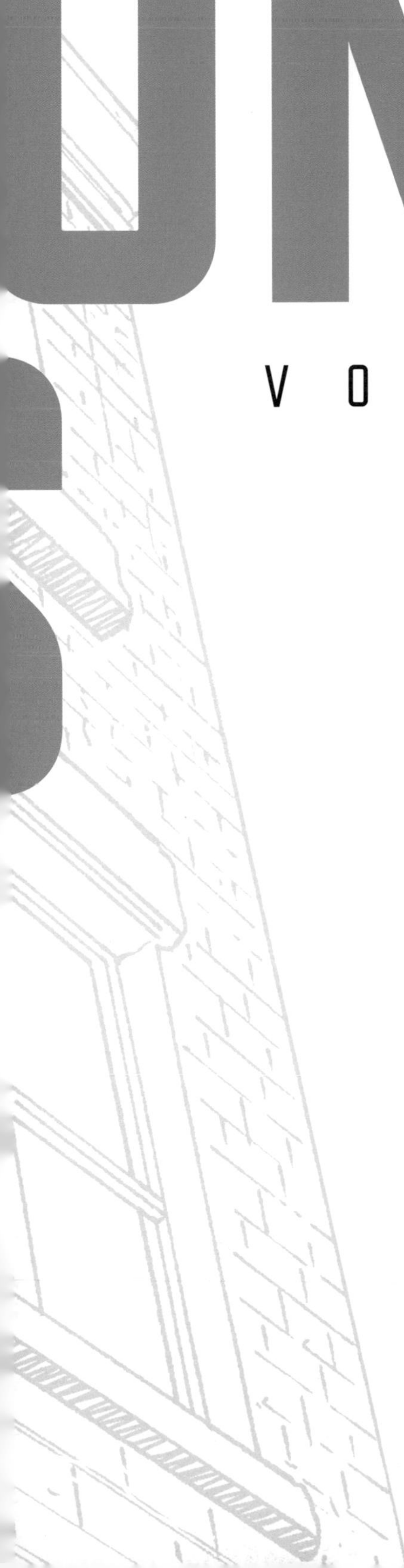

VERSION CONTROL

STORY | David A. Robertson

ART | Scott B. Henderson

COLOURS | Donovan Yaciuk

LETTERS | Andrew Thomas

HIGHWATER PRESS

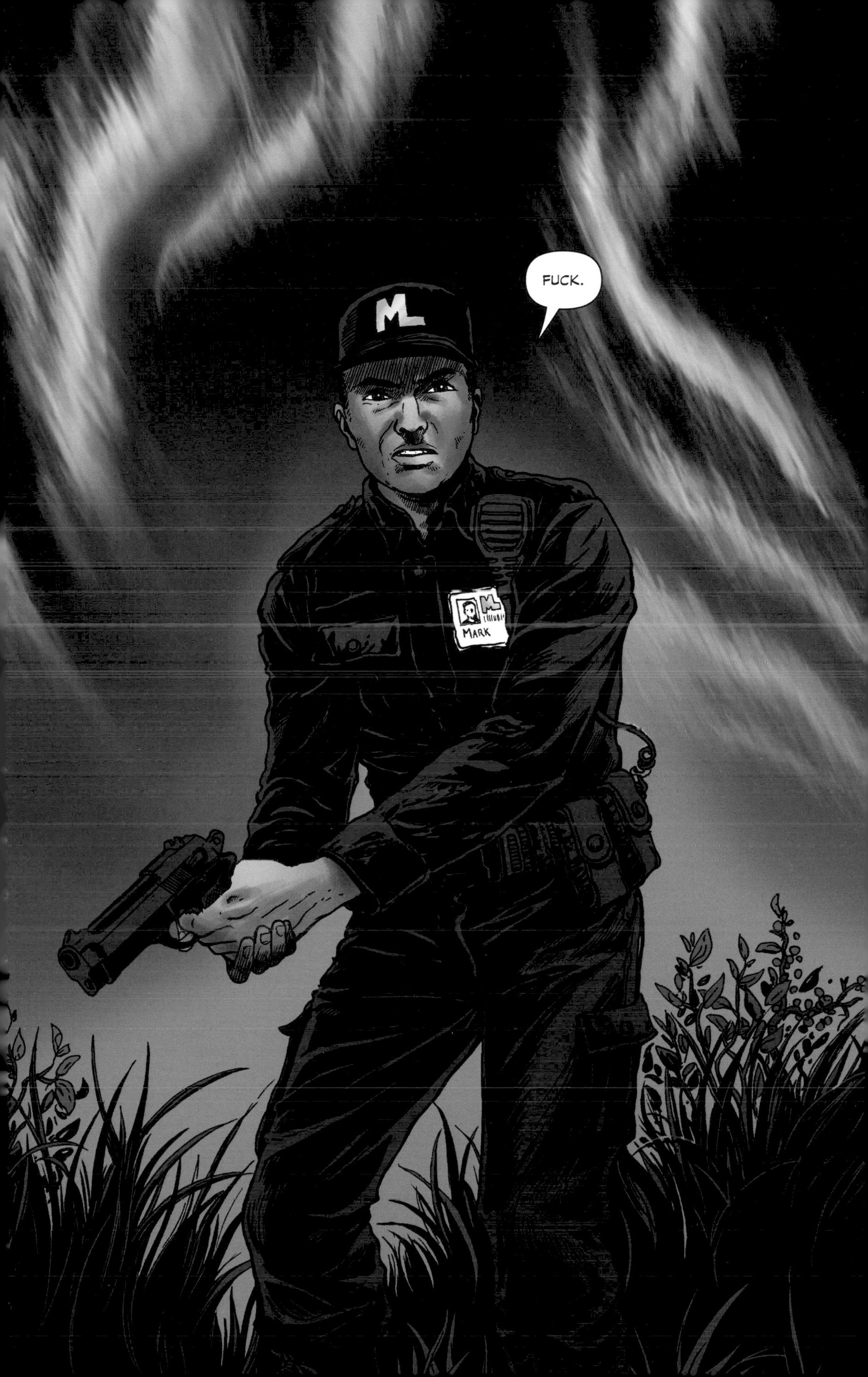
FUCK.
MARK

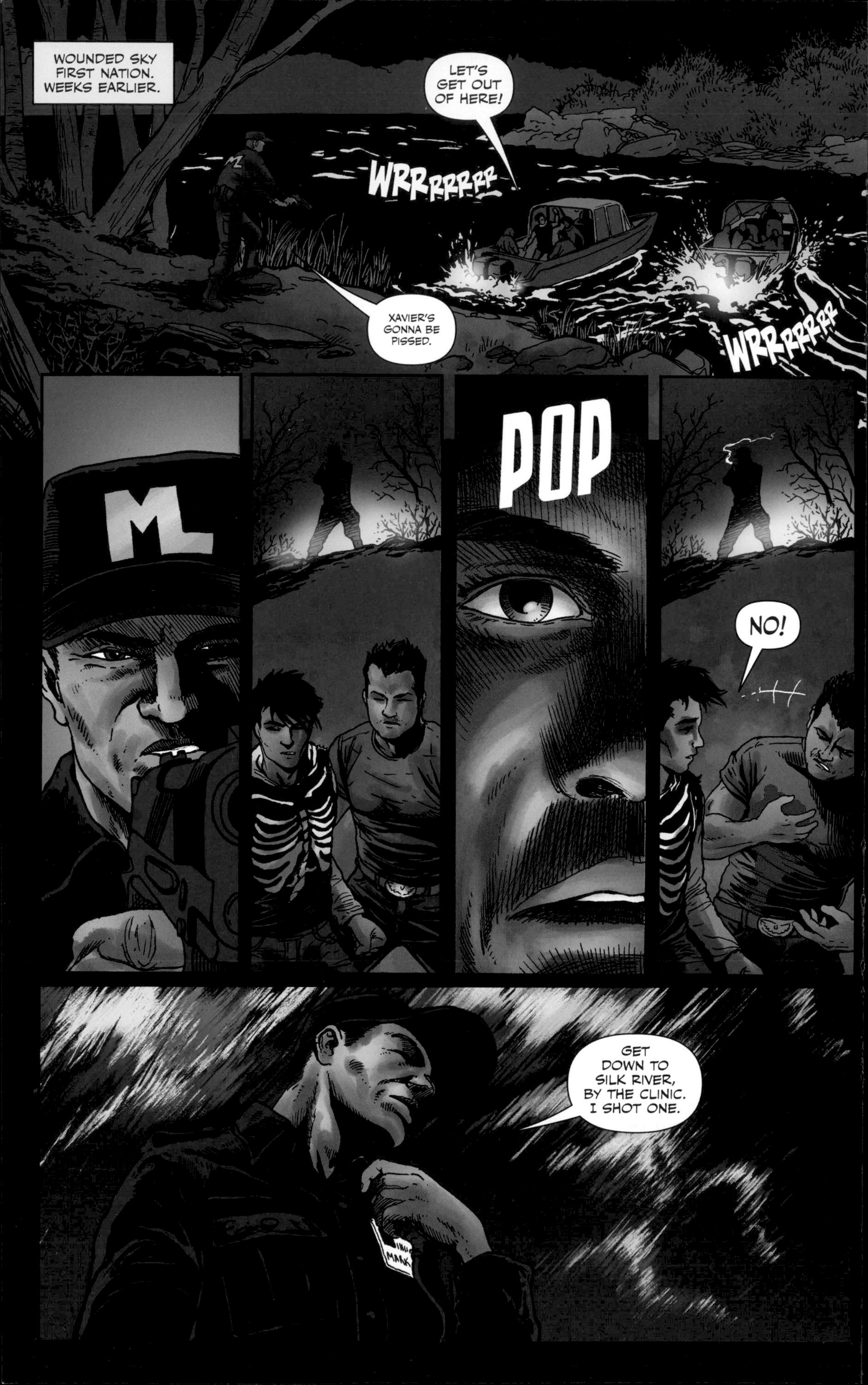
WOUNDED SKY FIRST NATION. WEEKS EARLIER.
LET'S GET OUT OF HERE!
WRRRRRRR
XAVIER'S GONNA BE PISSED.
WRRRRRRR
ML
POP
NO!
GET DOWN TO SILK RIVER, BY THE CLINIC. I SHOT ONE.

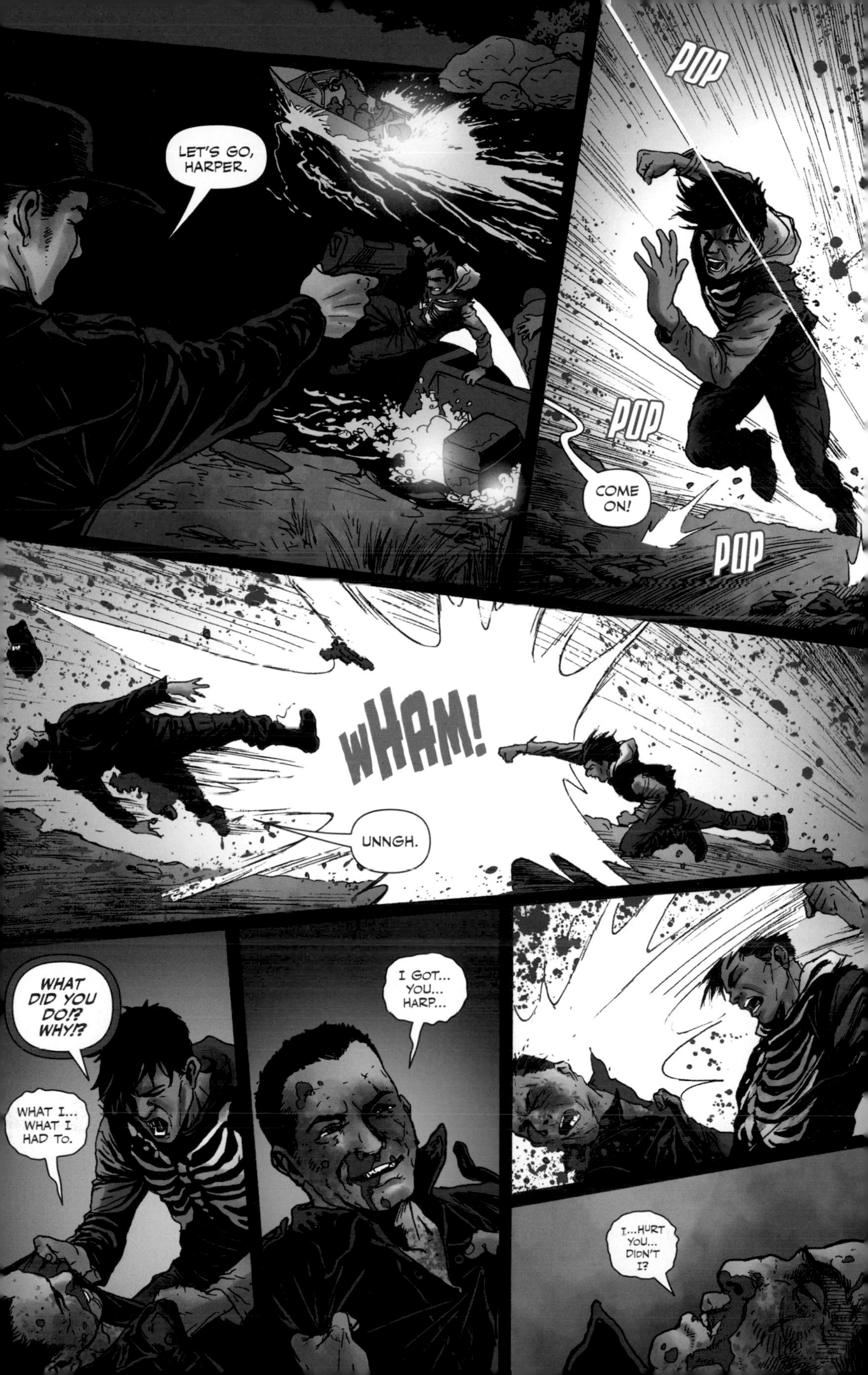
LET'S GO, HARPER.
POP
POP
COME ON!
POP
WHAM!
UNNGH.
WHAT DID YOU DO!? WHY!?
WHAT I... WHAT I HAD TO.
I GOT... YOU... HARP...
I...HURT YOU... DIDN'T I?

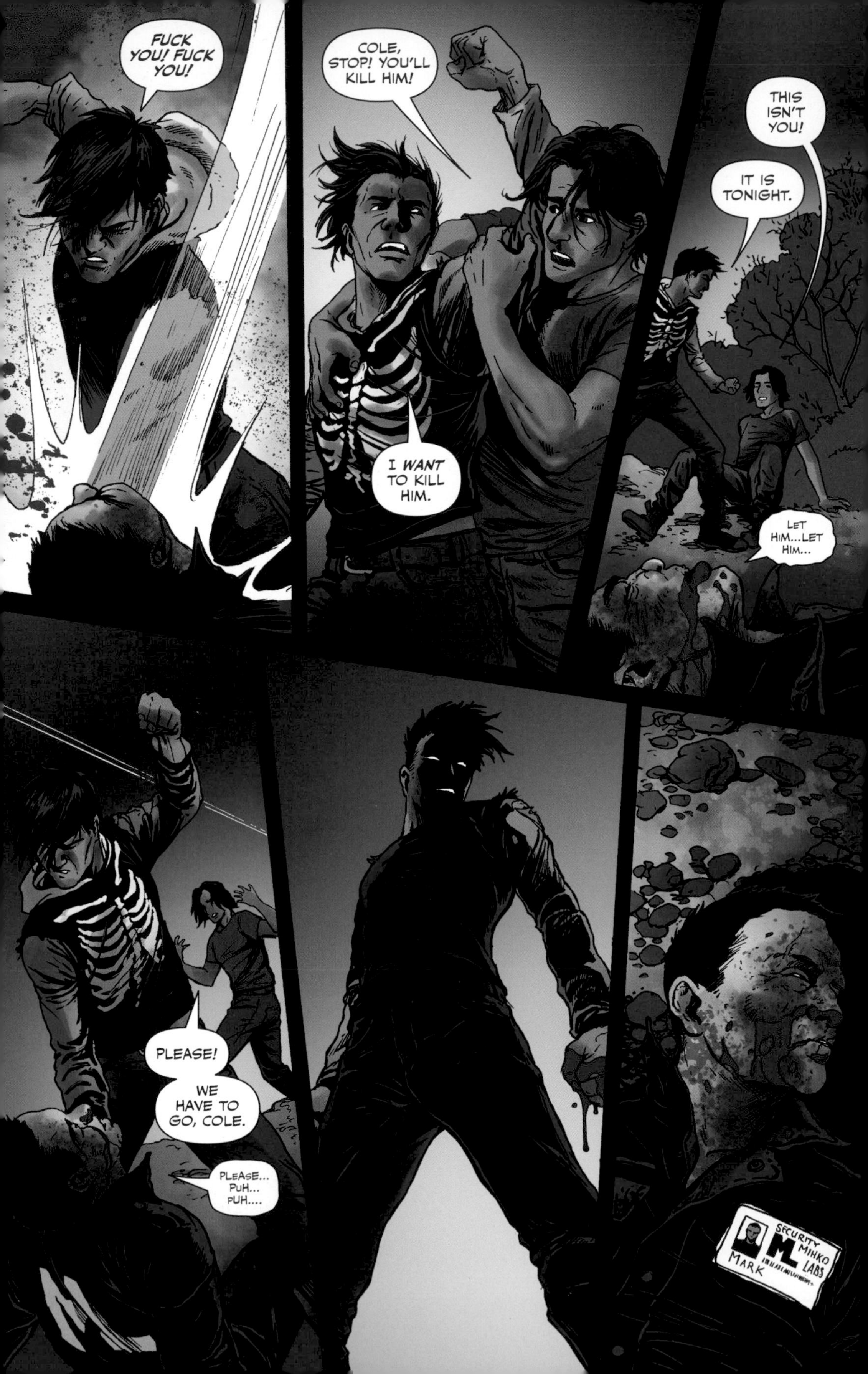
FUCK YOU! FUCK YOU!
COLE, STOP! YOU'LL KILL HIM!
I *WANT* TO KILL HIM.
THIS ISN'T YOU!
IT IS TONIGHT.
LET HIM...LET HIM...
PLEASE!
WE HAVE TO GO, COLE.
PLEASE... PUH... PUH....
SECURITY
MIHKO LABS
MARK

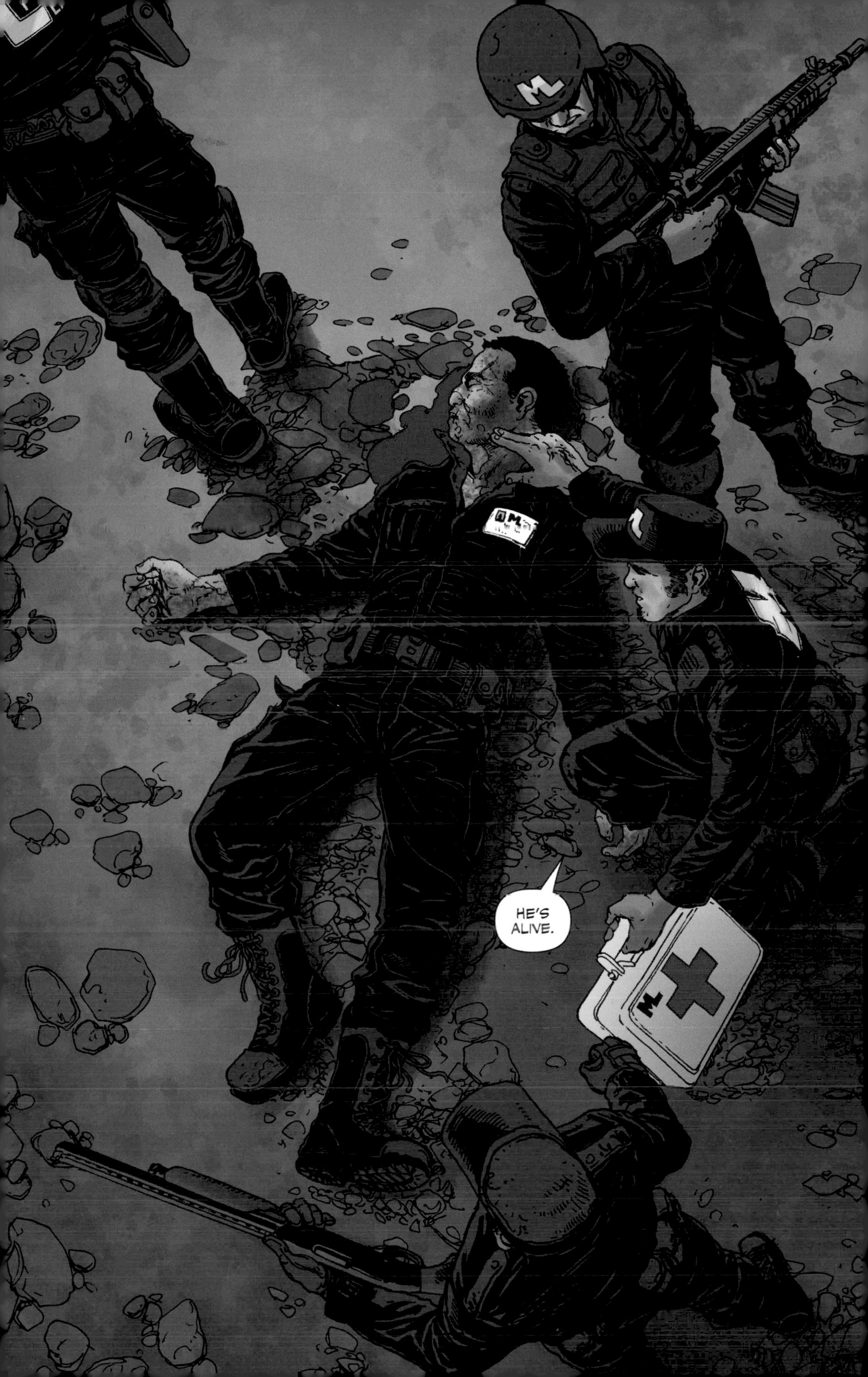
HE'S ALIVE.

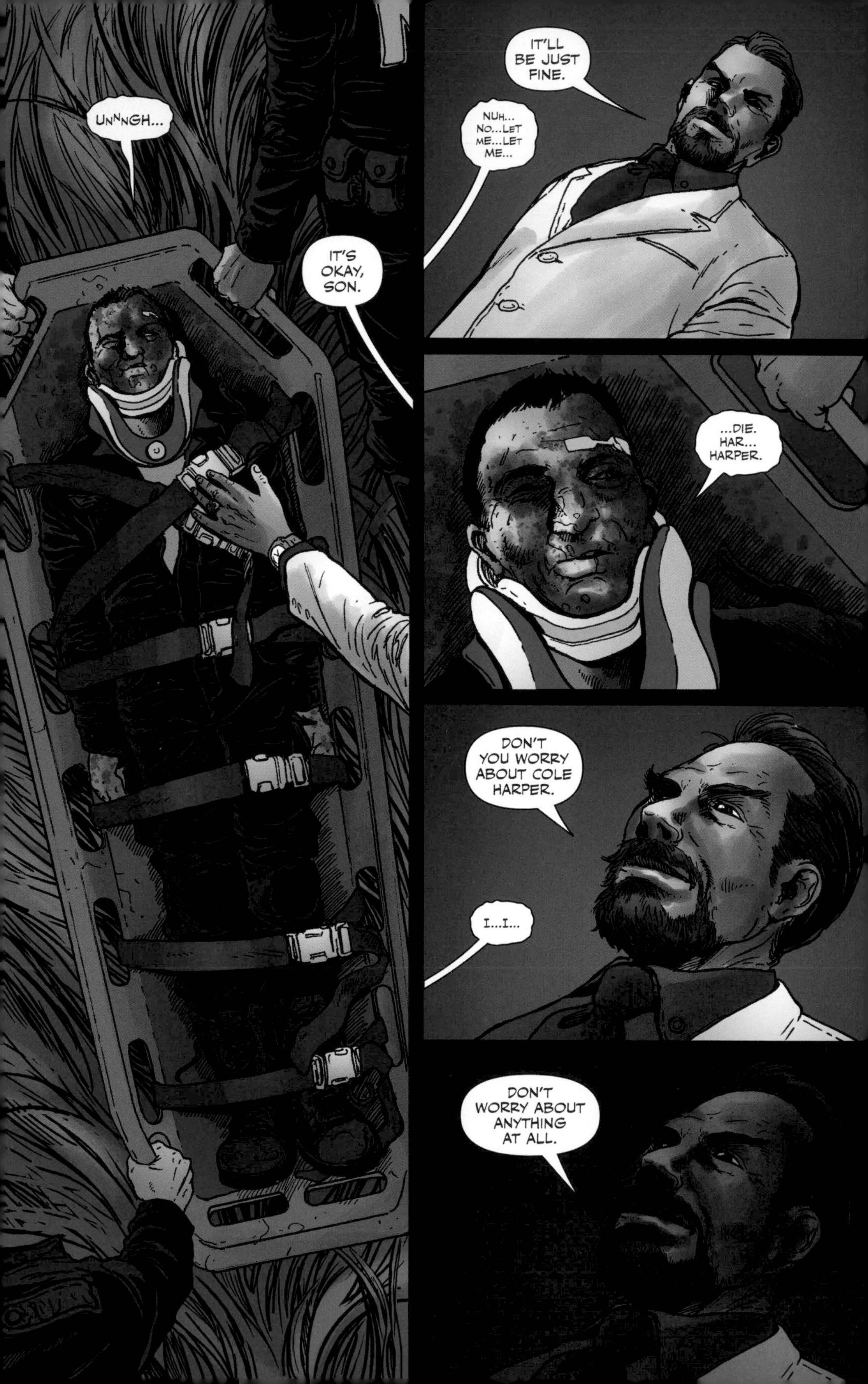
UNNNGH...
IT'S OKAY, SON.
IT'LL BE JUST FINE.
NUH... NO...LET ME...LET ME...
...DIE. HAR... HARPER.
DON'T YOU WORRY ABOUT COLE HARPER.
I...I...
DON'T WORRY ABOUT ANYTHING AT ALL.

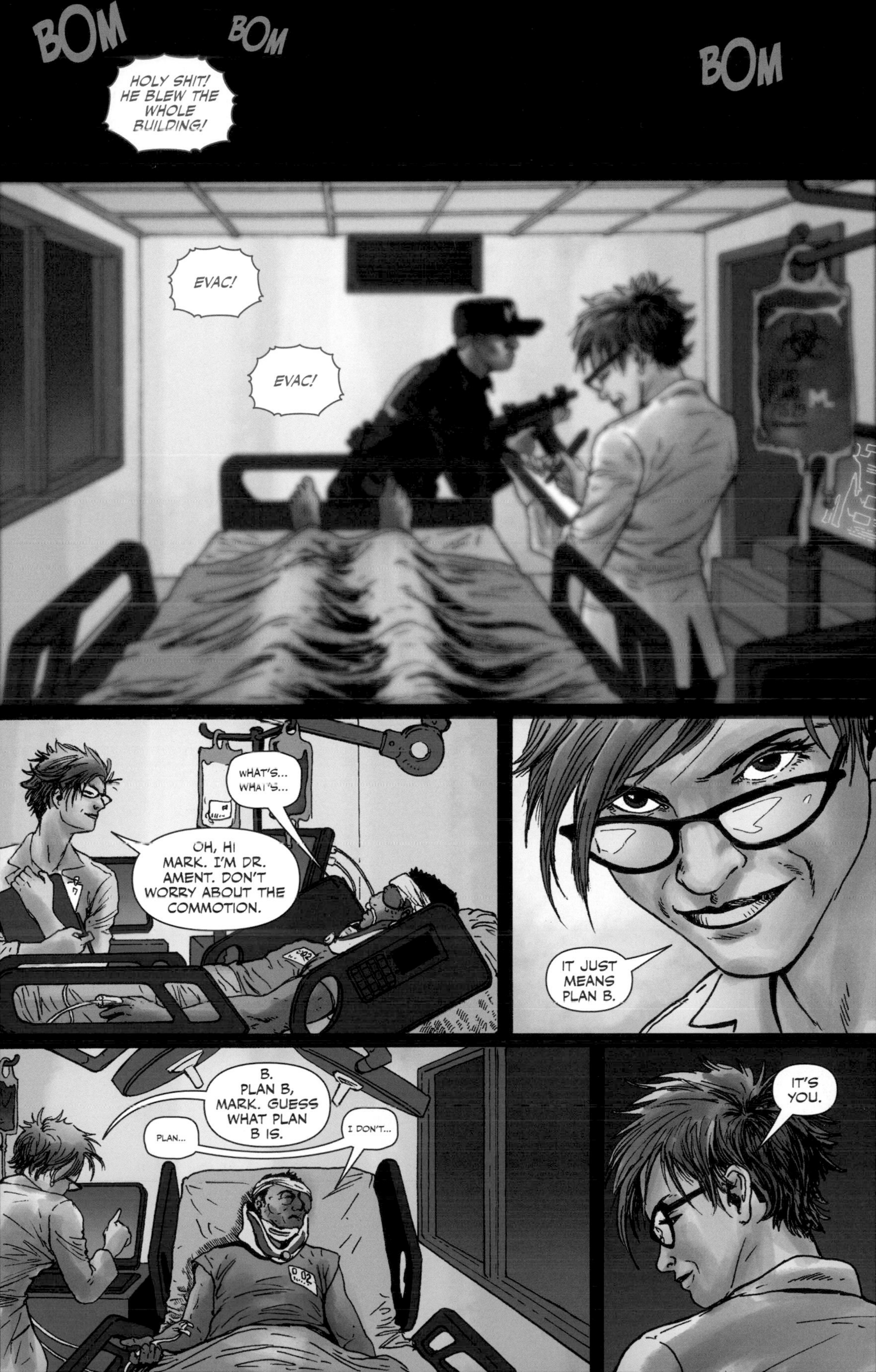
BOM
BOM
BOM
HOLY SHIT! HE BLEW THE WHOLE BUILDING!
EVAC!
EVAC!
WHAT'S... WHAT'S...
OH, HI MARK. I'M DR. AMENT. DON'T WORRY ABOUT THE COMMOTION.
IT JUST MEANS PLAN B.
PLAN...
B. PLAN B, MARK. GUESS WHAT PLAN B IS.
I DON'T...
IT'S YOU.

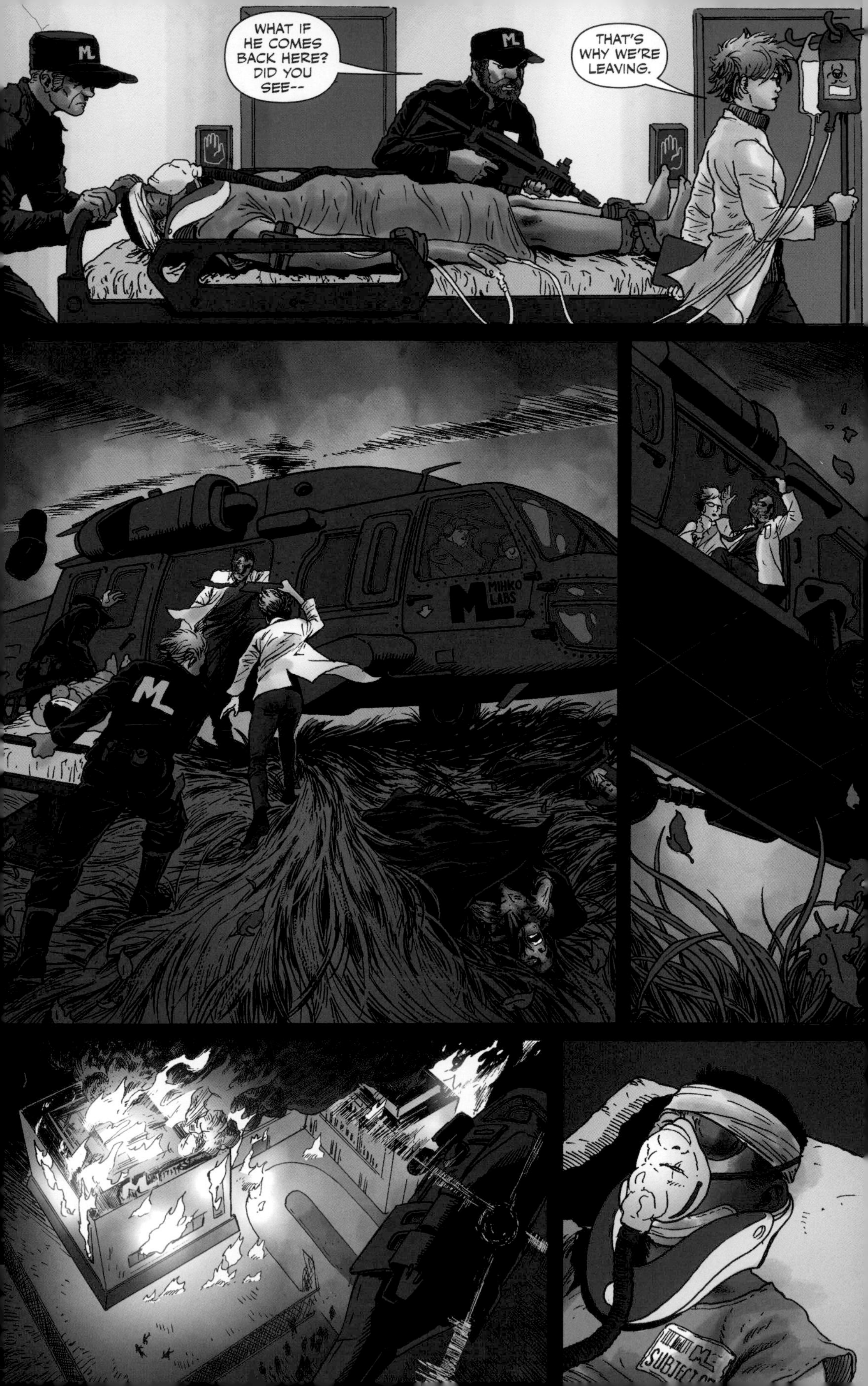
WHAT IF HE COMES BACK HERE? DID YOU SEE--
THAT'S WHY WE'RE LEAVING.
MIHKO LABS
SUBJECT

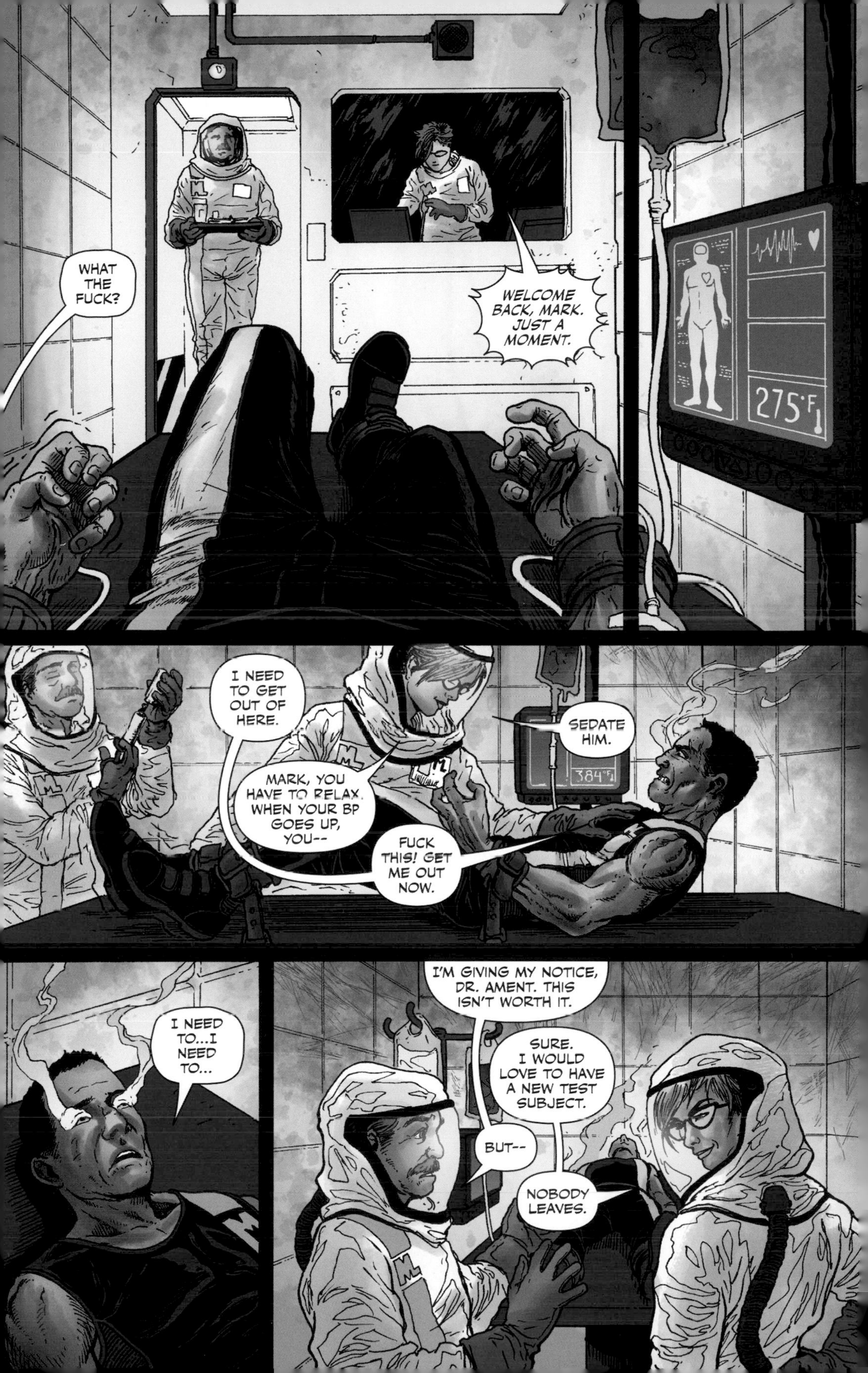
WHAT THE FUCK?
WELCOME BACK, MARK. JUST A MOMENT.
275°F
I NEED TO GET OUT OF HERE.
SEDATE HIM.
384°F
MARK, YOU HAVE TO RELAX. WHEN YOUR BP GOES UP, YOU--
FUCK THIS! GET ME OUT NOW.
I NEED TO...I NEED TO...
I'M GIVING MY NOTICE, DR. AMENT. THIS ISN'T WORTH IT.
SURE. I WOULD LOVE TO HAVE A NEW TEST SUBJECT.
BUT--
NOBODY LEAVES.

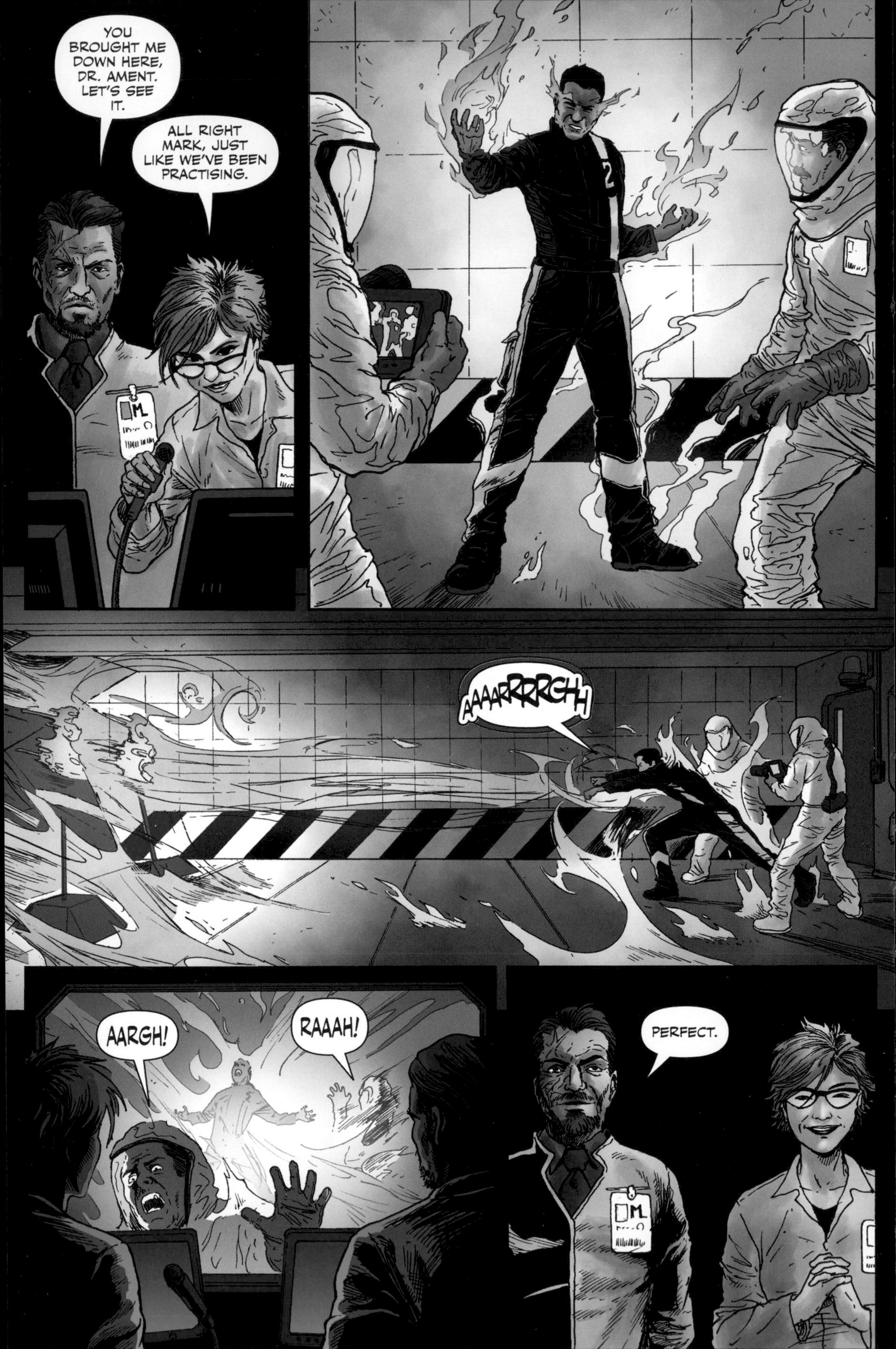
YOU BROUGHT ME DOWN HERE, DR. AMENT. LET'S SEE IT.
ALL RIGHT MARK, JUST LIKE WE'VE BEEN PRACTISING.
AAAARRRRGHH
AARGH!
RAAAH!
PERFECT.

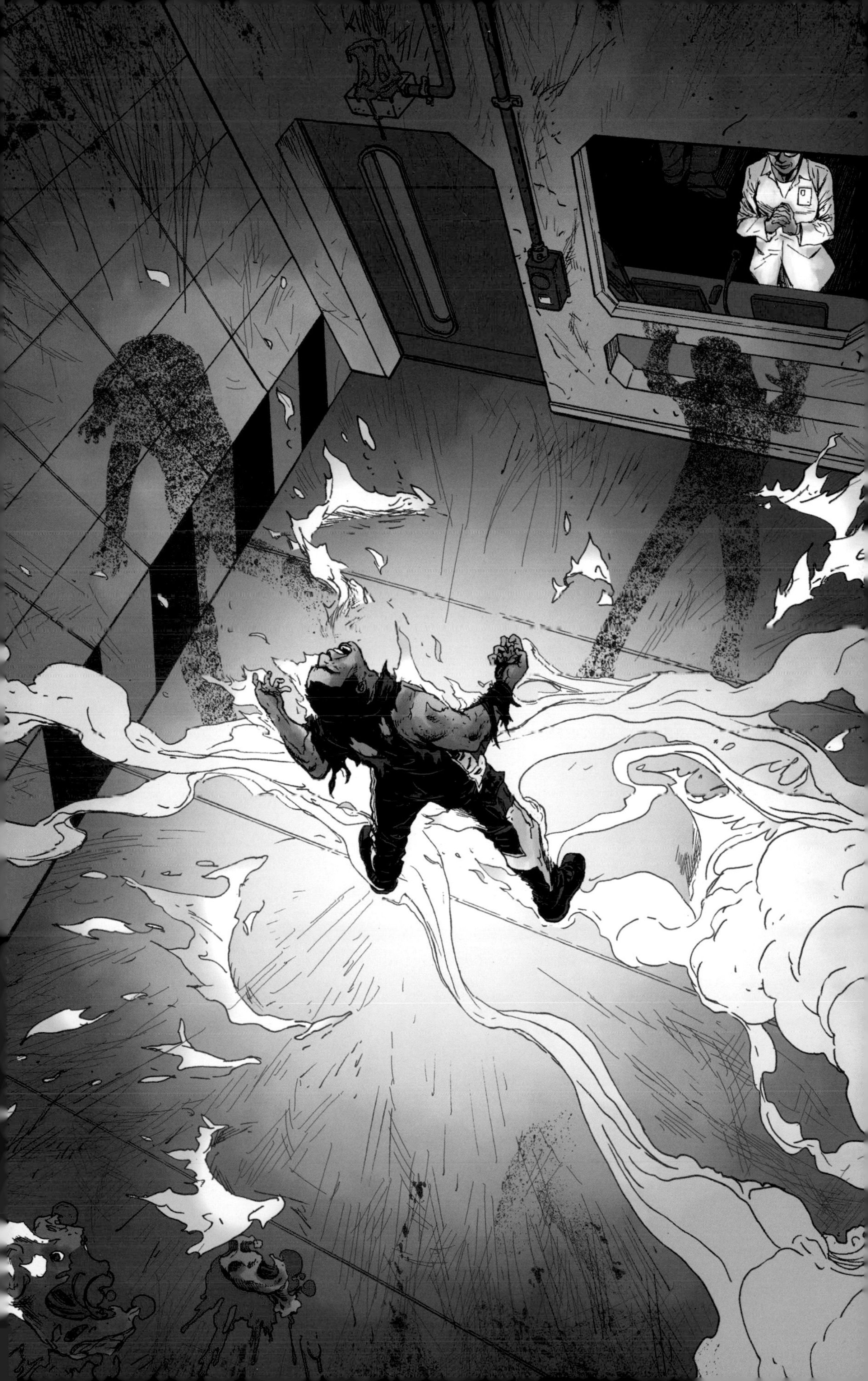

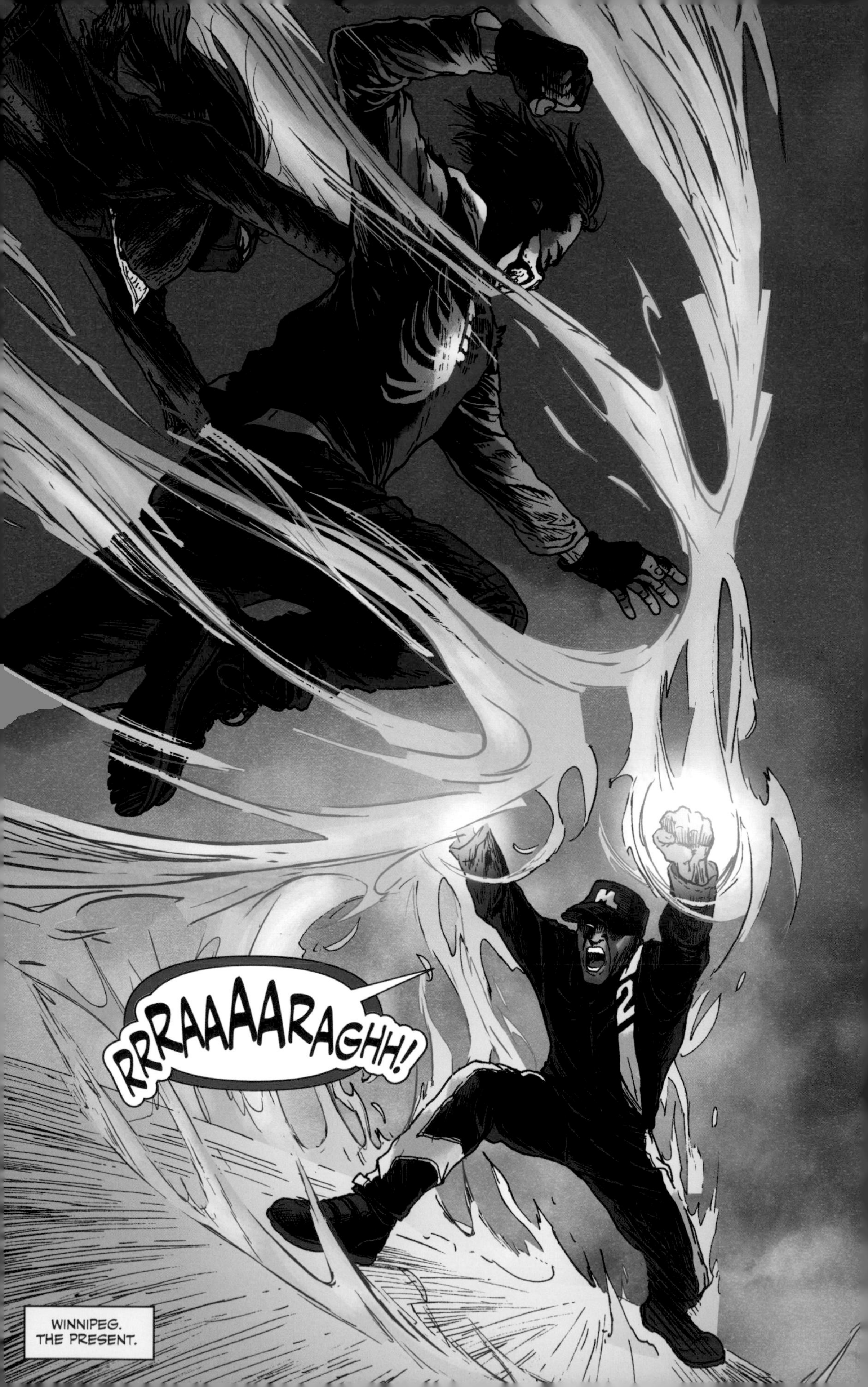
RRRAAAARAGHH!
WINNIPEG.
THE PRESENT.

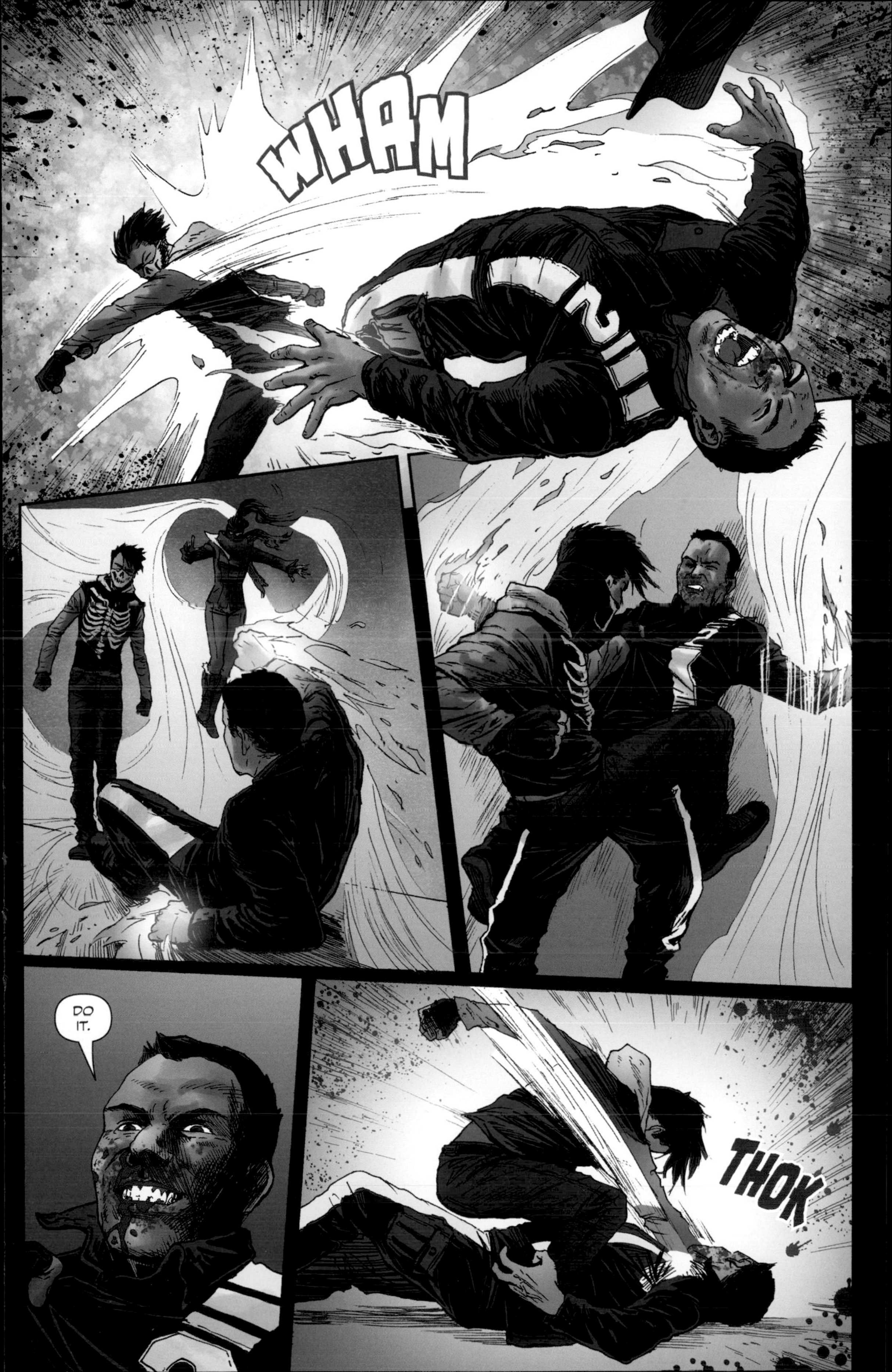
WHAM
DO IT.
THOK

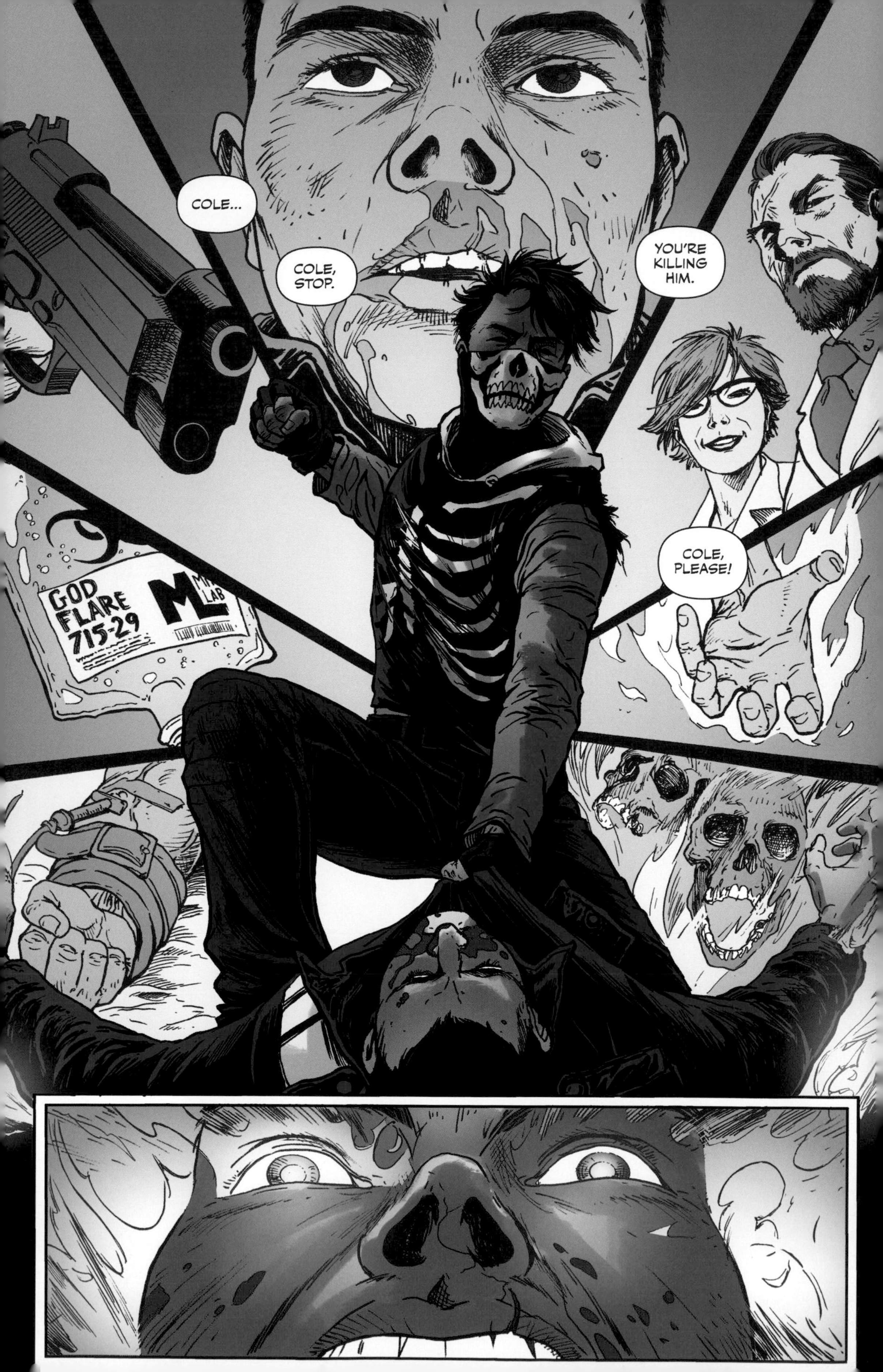
COLE...
COLE, STOP.
YOU'RE KILLING HIM.
COLE, PLEASE!
GOD FLARE 715-29
ML

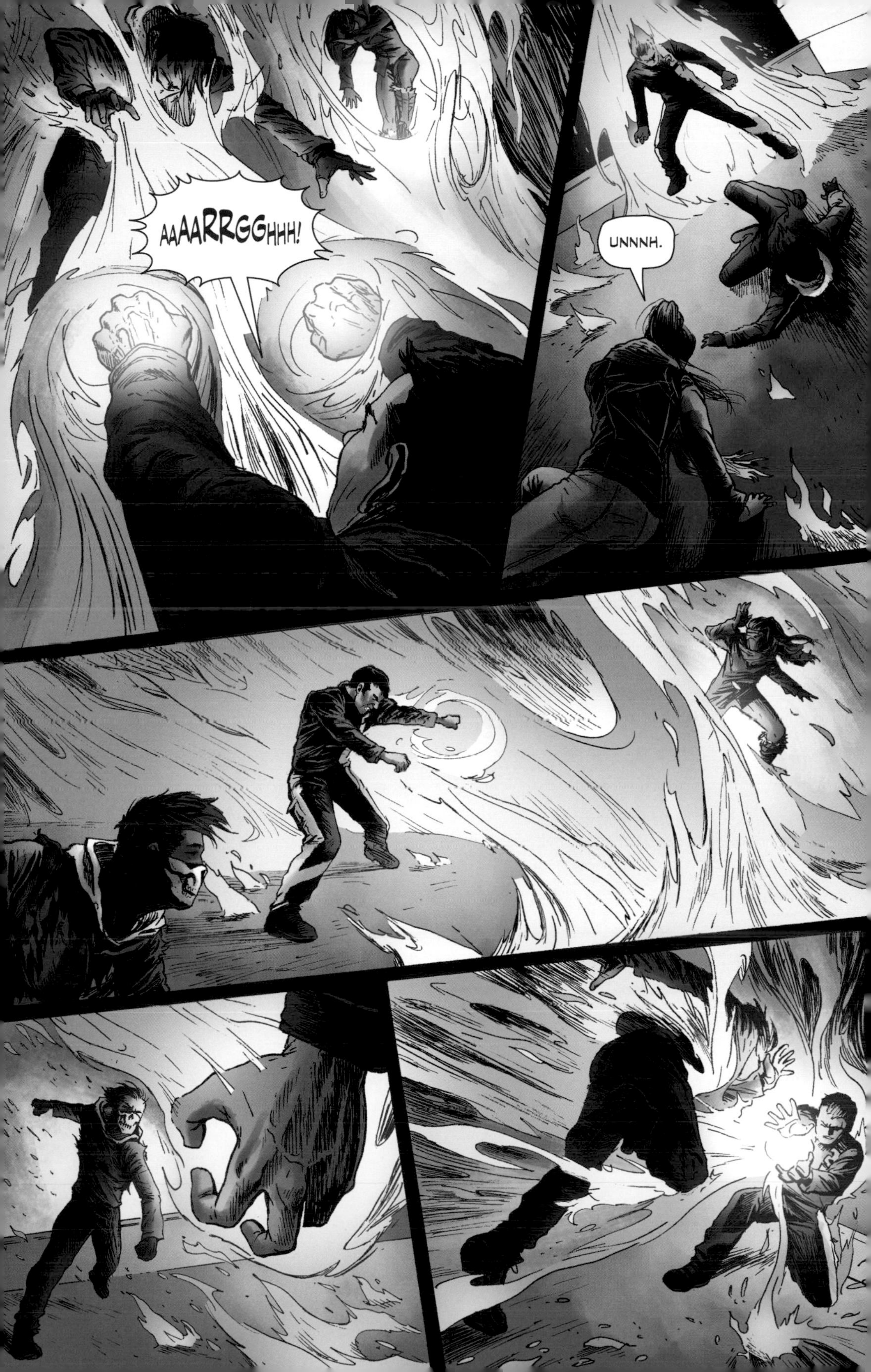
AAAARRGGHHH!
UNNNH.

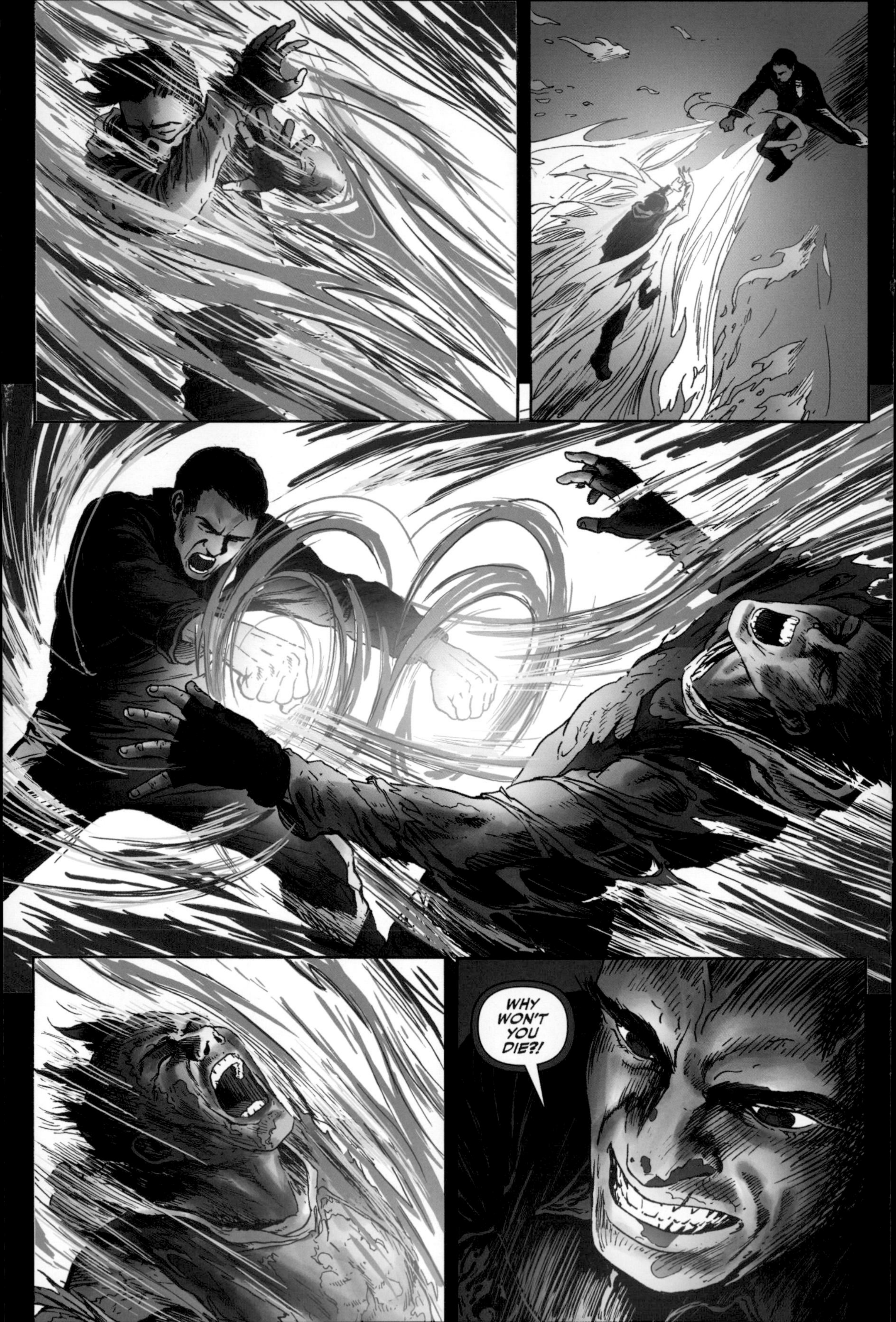
WHY WON'T YOU DIE?!

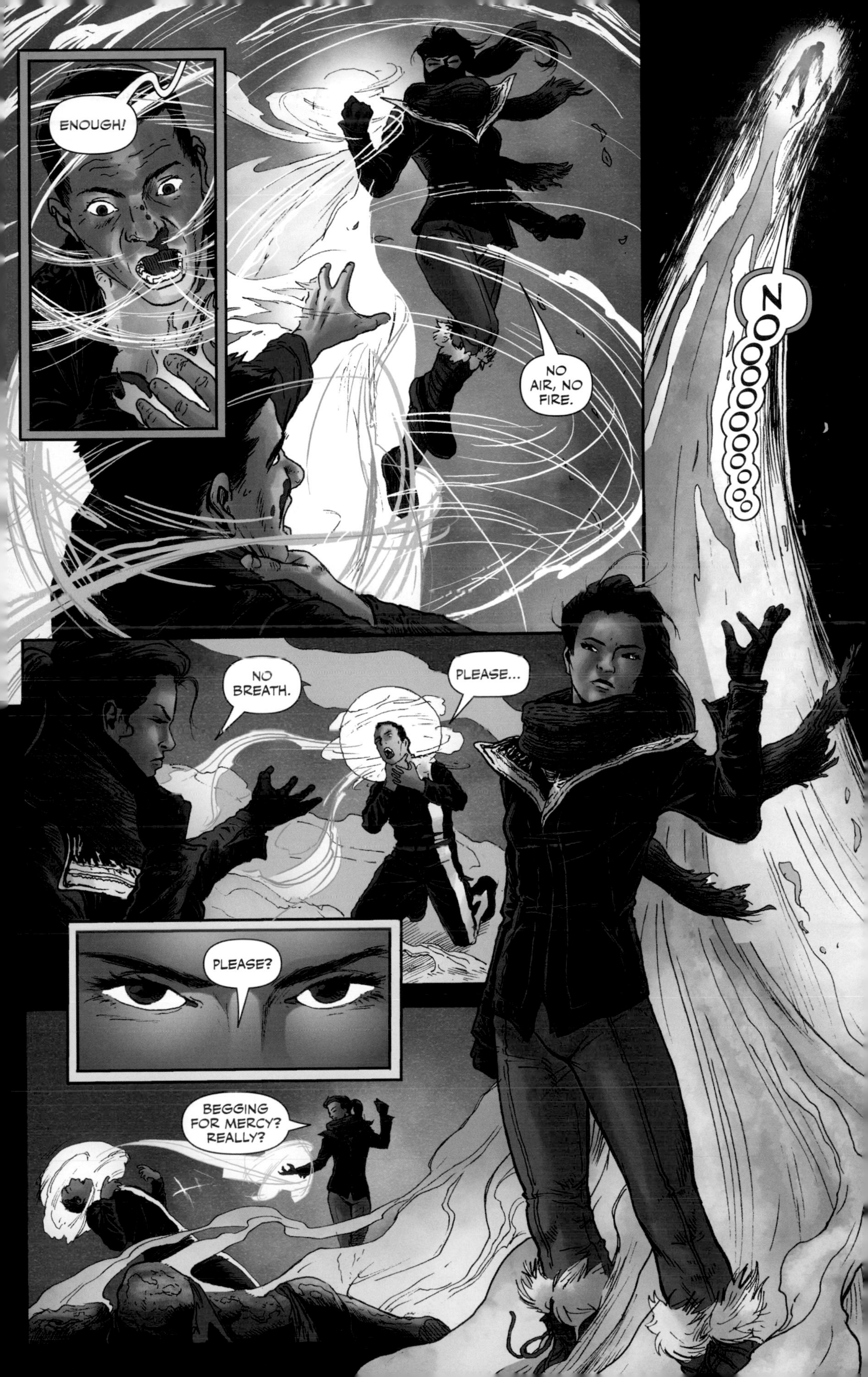
ENOUGH!
NO AIR, NO FIRE.
NOOOOOOOOOOOO
NO BREATH.
PLEASE...
PLEASE?
BEGGING FOR MERCY? REALLY?

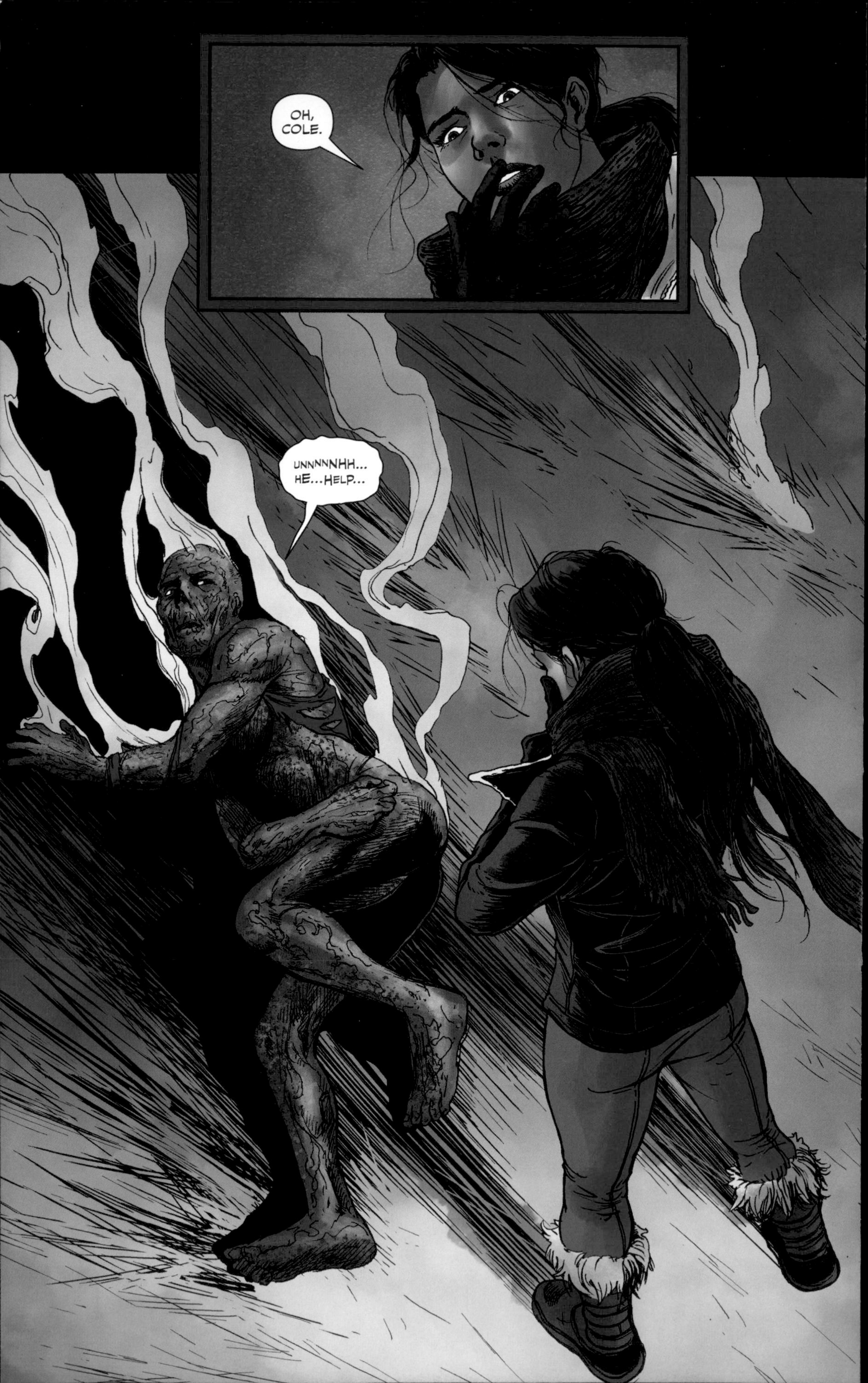
OH, COLE.
UNNNNHH... HE...HELP...

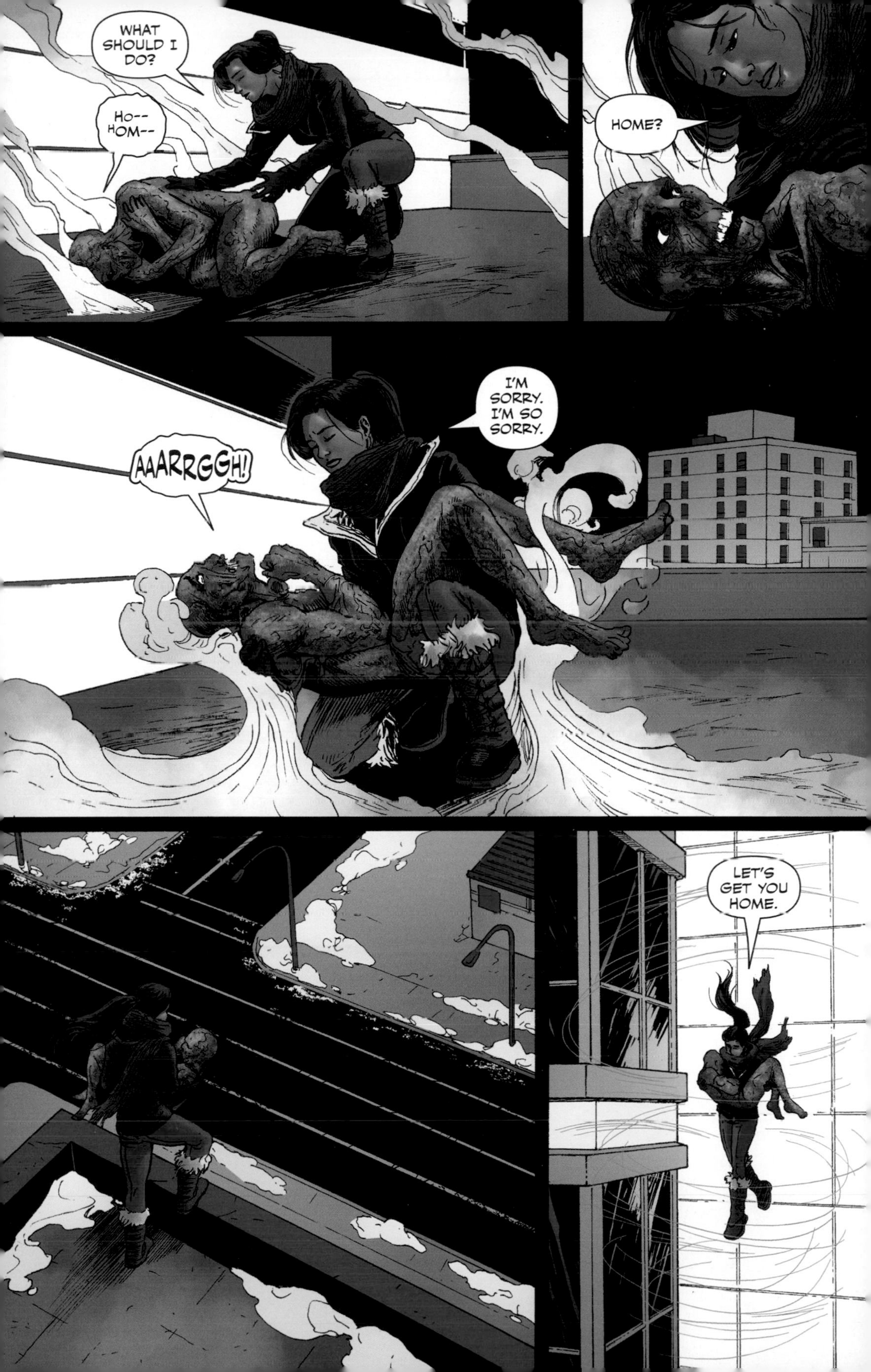
WHAT SHOULD I DO?
HO-- HOM--
HOME?
AAARRGGH!
I'M SORRY. I'M SO SORRY.
LET'S GET YOU HOME.

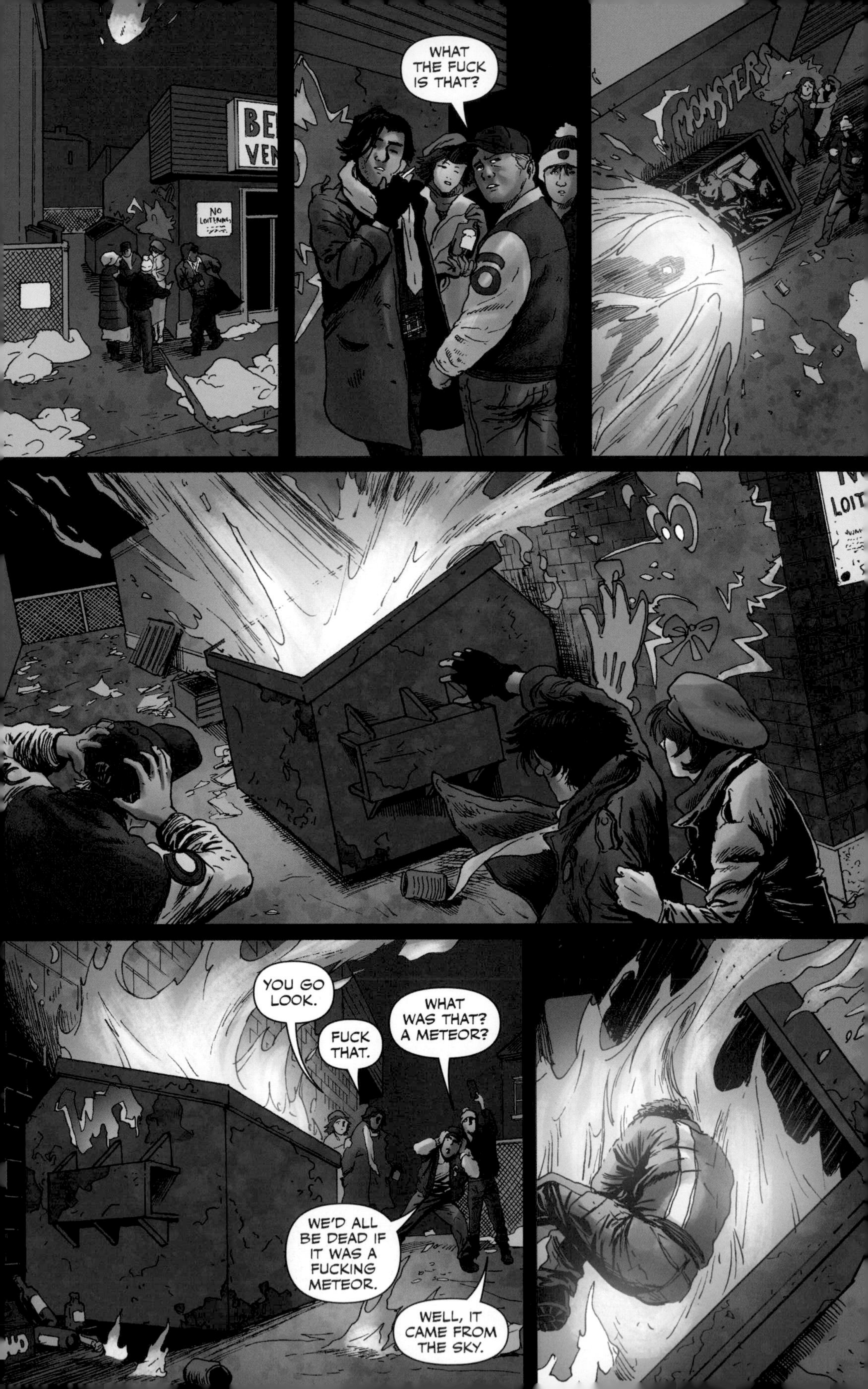
NO LOITERING
WHAT THE FUCK IS THAT?
MONSTERS
YOU GO LOOK.
FUCK THAT.
WHAT WAS THAT? A METEOR?
WE'D ALL BE DEAD IF IT WAS A FUCKING METEOR.
WELL, IT CAME FROM THE SKY.

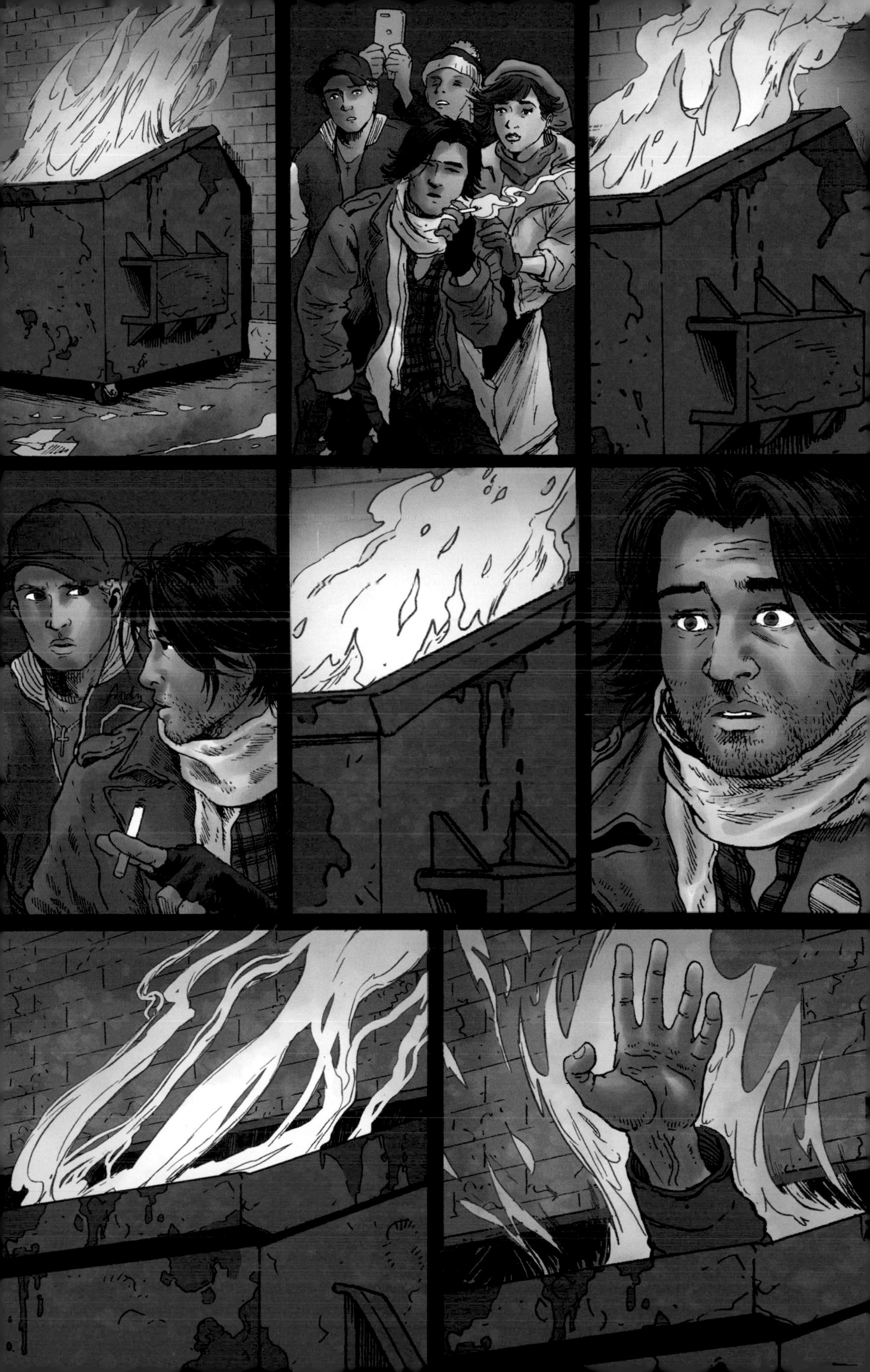

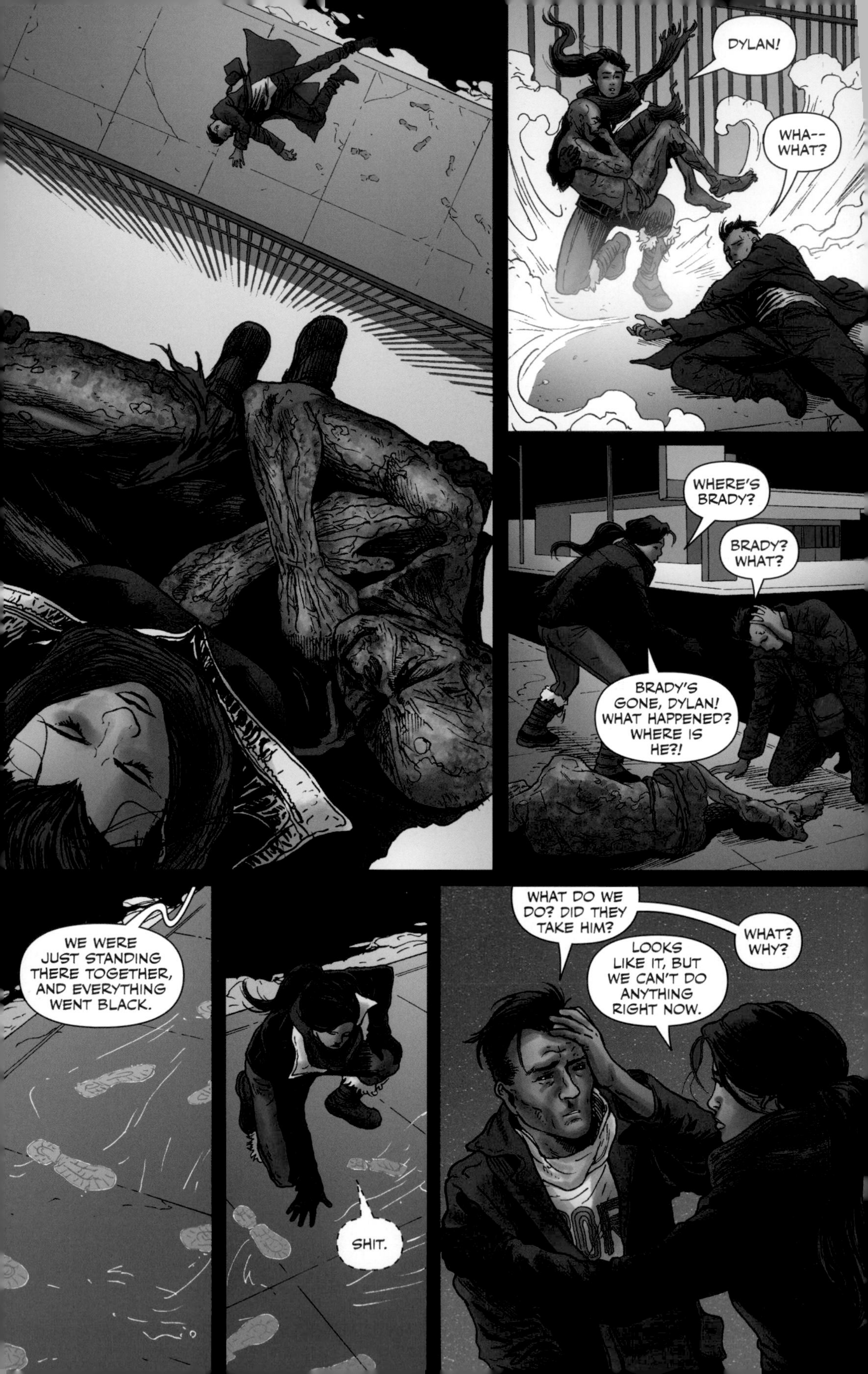
DYLAN!
WHA--
WHAT?
WHERE'S
BRADY?
BRADY?
WHAT?
BRADY'S
GONE, DYLAN!
WHAT HAPPENED?
WHERE IS
HE?!
WE WERE
JUST STANDING
THERE TOGETHER,
AND EVERYTHING
WENT BLACK.
SHIT.
WHAT DO WE
DO? DID THEY
TAKE HIM?
WHAT?
WHY?
LOOKS
LIKE IT, BUT
WE CAN'T DO
ANYTHING
RIGHT NOW.

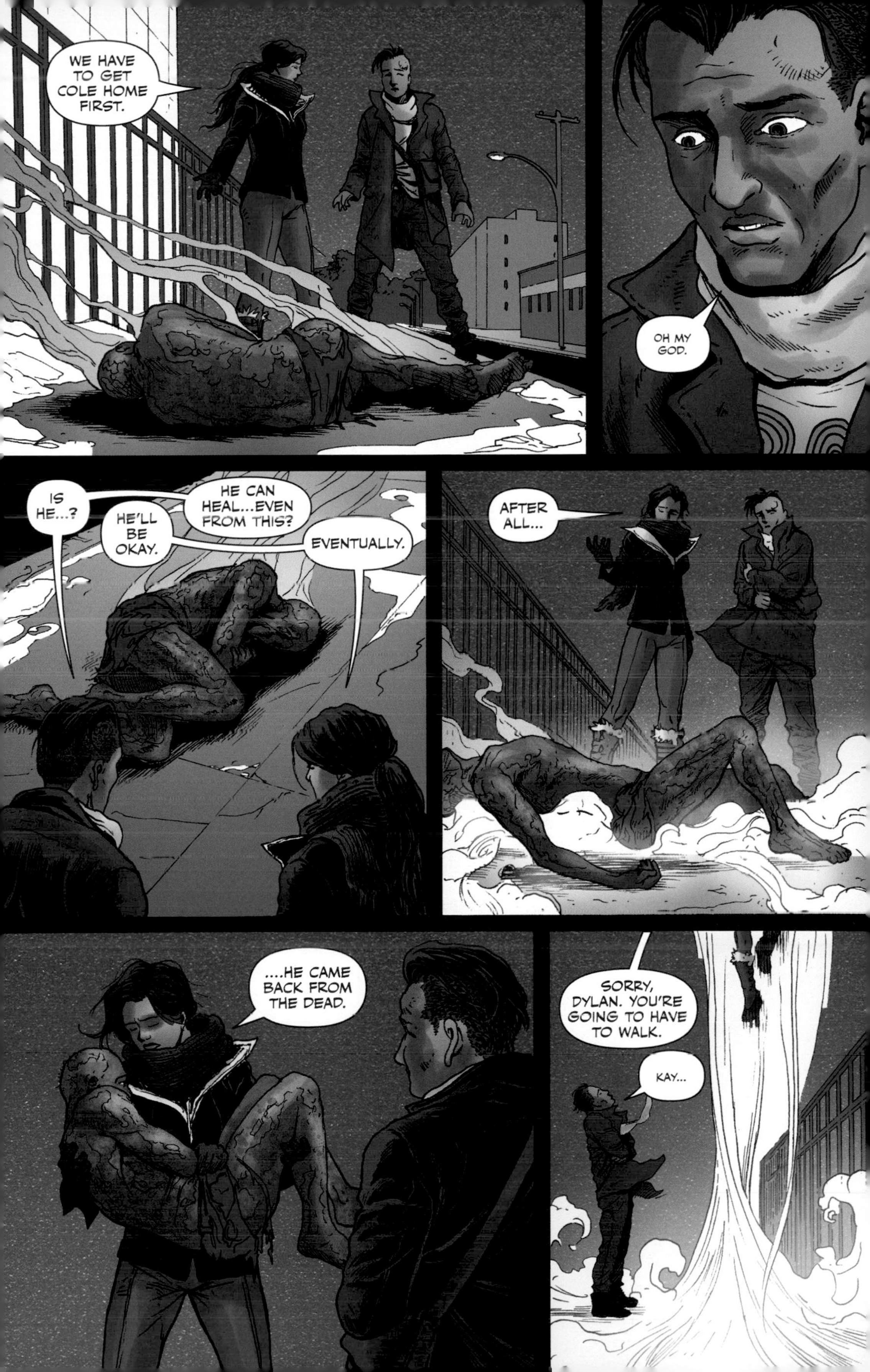
WE HAVE TO GET COLE HOME FIRST.
OH MY GOD.
IS HE...?
HE'LL BE OKAY.
HE CAN HEAL...EVEN FROM THIS?
EVENTUALLY.
AFTER ALL...
....HE CAME BACK FROM THE DEAD.
SORRY, DYLAN. YOU'RE GOING TO HAVE TO WALK.
KAY...

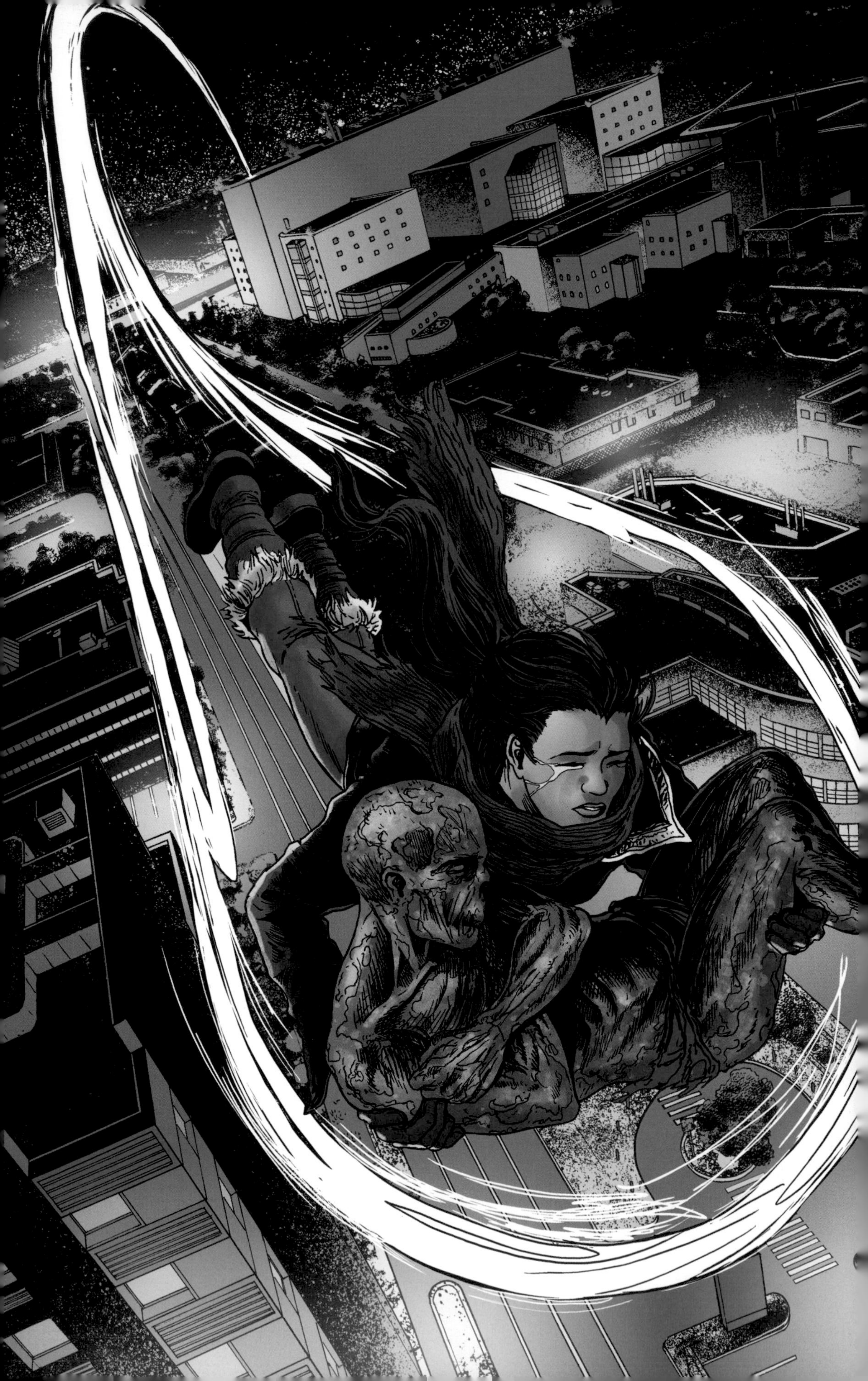

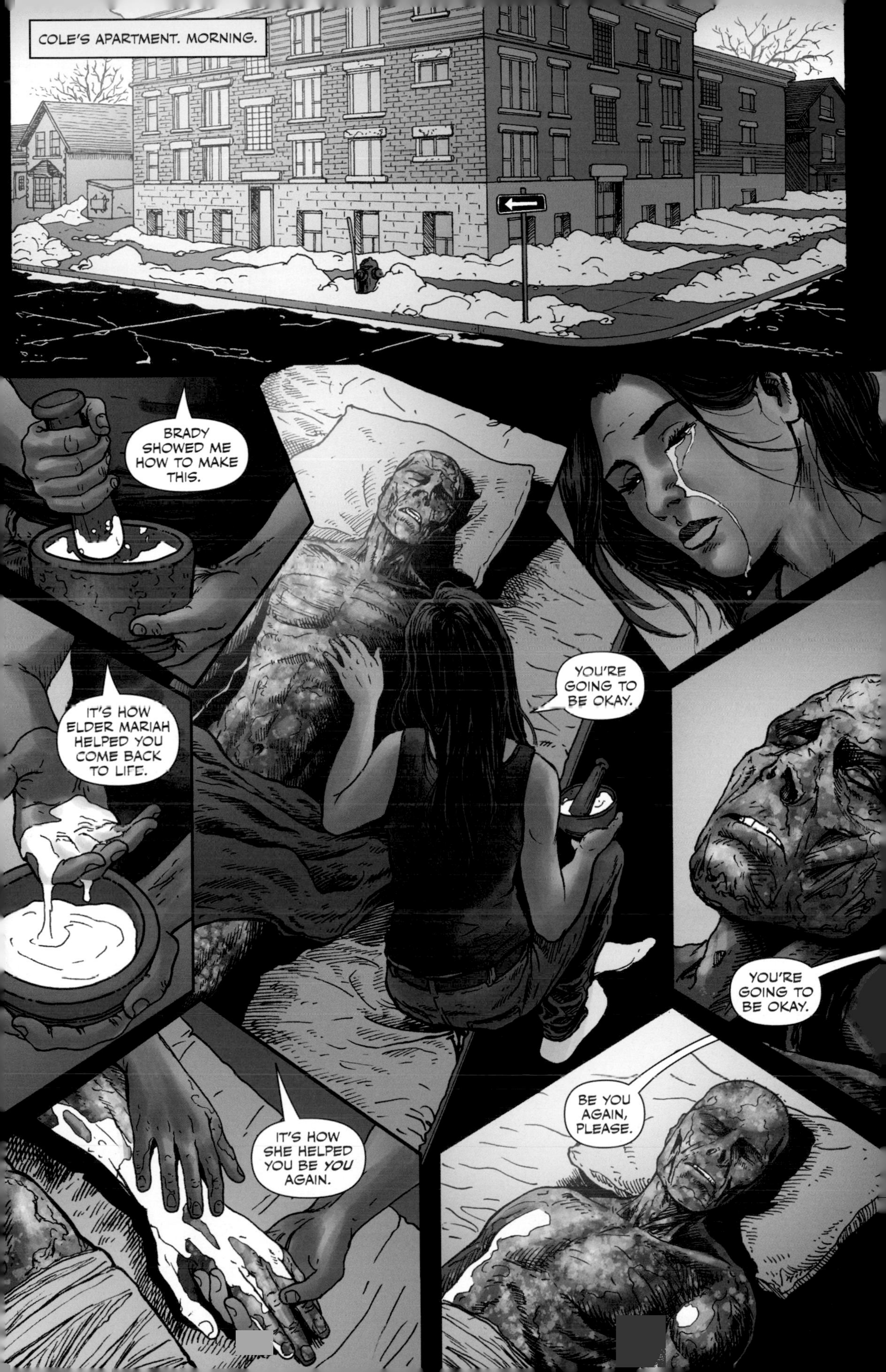
COLE'S APARTMENT. MORNING.
BRADY SHOWED ME HOW TO MAKE THIS.
IT'S HOW ELDER MARIAH HELPED YOU COME BACK TO LIFE.
YOU'RE GOING TO BE OKAY.
YOU'RE GOING TO BE OKAY.
IT'S HOW SHE HELPED YOU BE *YOU* AGAIN.
BE YOU AGAIN, PLEASE.

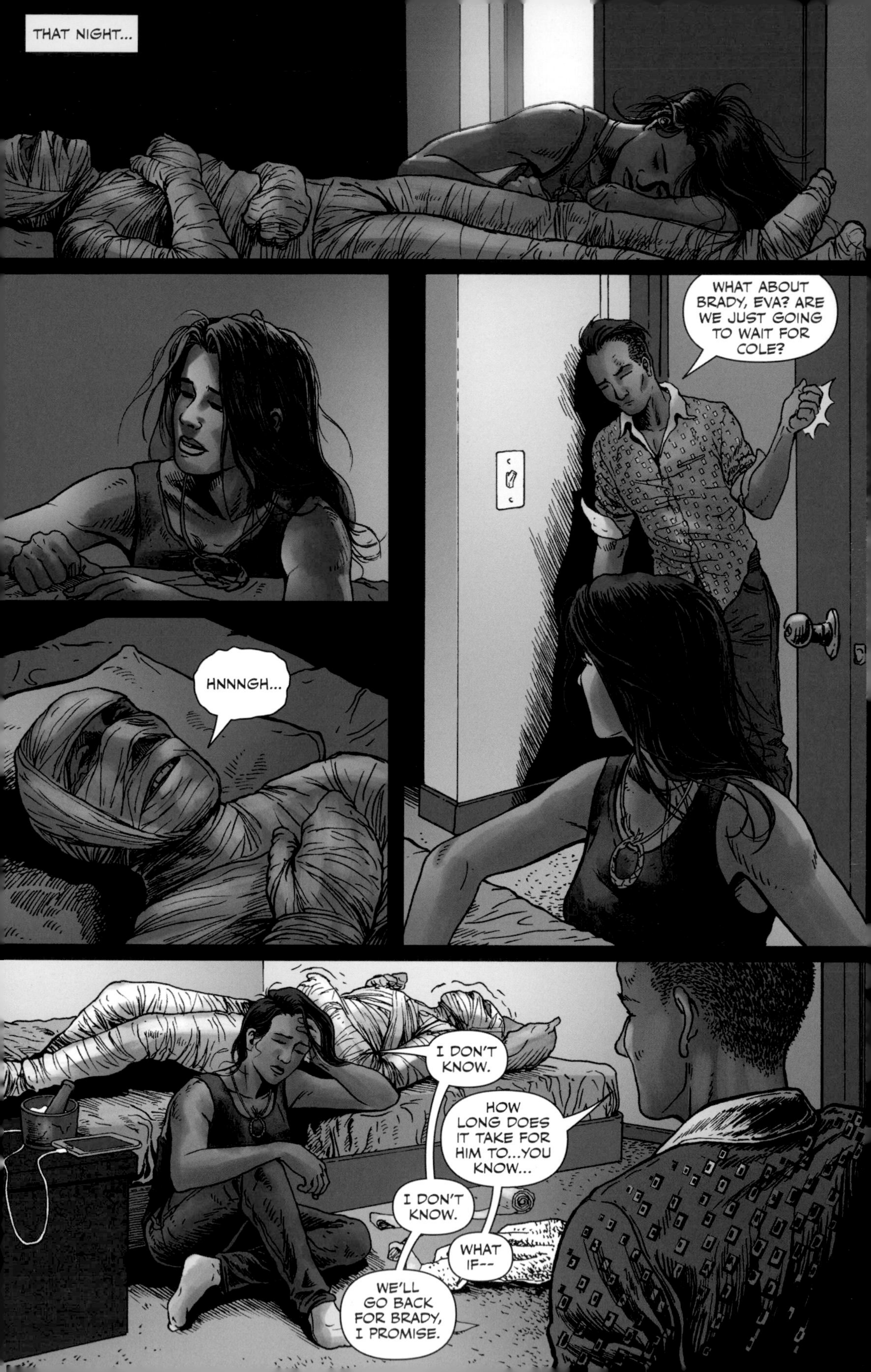
THAT NIGHT...
WHAT ABOUT BRADY, EVA? ARE WE JUST GOING TO WAIT FOR COLE?
HNNNGH...
I DON'T KNOW.
HOW LONG DOES IT TAKE FOR HIM TO...YOU KNOW...
I DON'T KNOW.
WHAT IF--
WE'LL GO BACK FOR BRADY, I PROMISE.

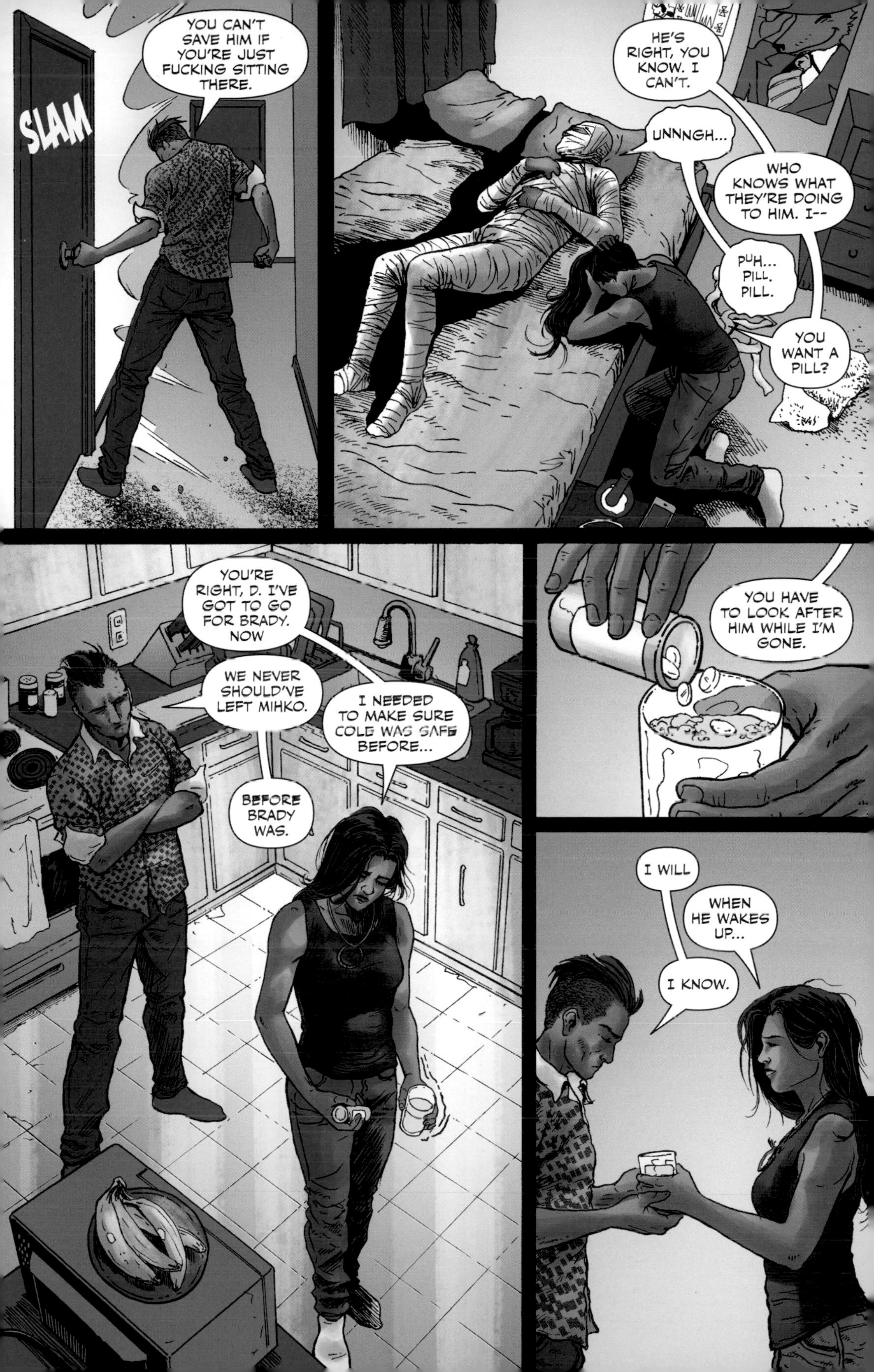
YOU CAN'T SAVE HIM IF YOU'RE JUST FUCKING SITTING THERE.
SLAM
HE'S RIGHT, YOU KNOW. I CAN'T.
UNNNGH...
WHO KNOWS WHAT THEY'RE DOING TO HIM. I--
PUH... PILL. PILL.
YOU WANT A PILL?
YOU'RE RIGHT, D. I'VE GOT TO GO FOR BRADY. NOW
WE NEVER SHOULD'VE LEFT MIHKO.
I NEEDED TO MAKE SURE COLE WAS SAFE BEFORE...
BEFORE BRADY WAS.
YOU HAVE TO LOOK AFTER HIM WHILE I'M GONE.
I WILL
WHEN HE WAKES UP...
I KNOW.

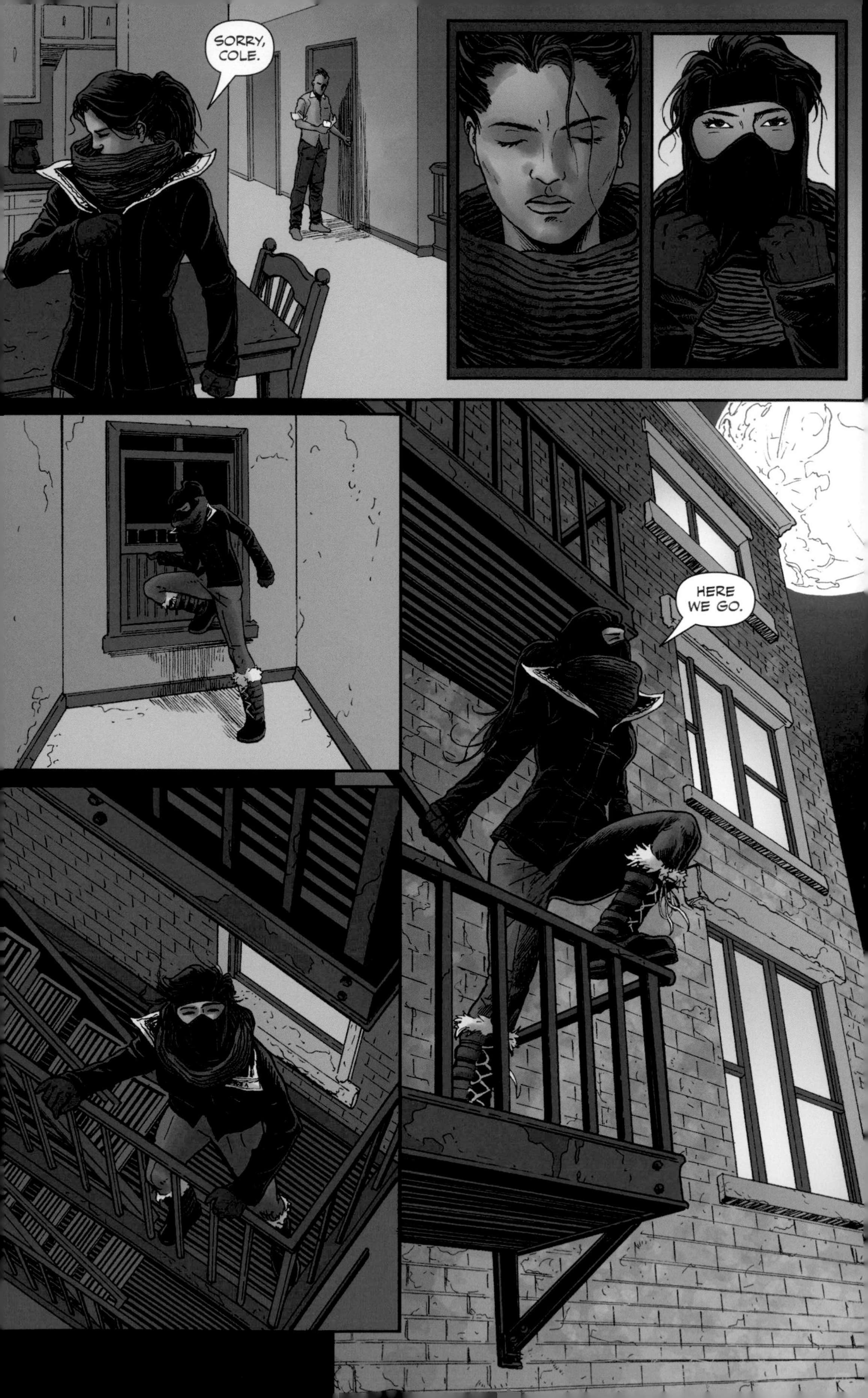
SORRY, COLE.
HERE WE GO.

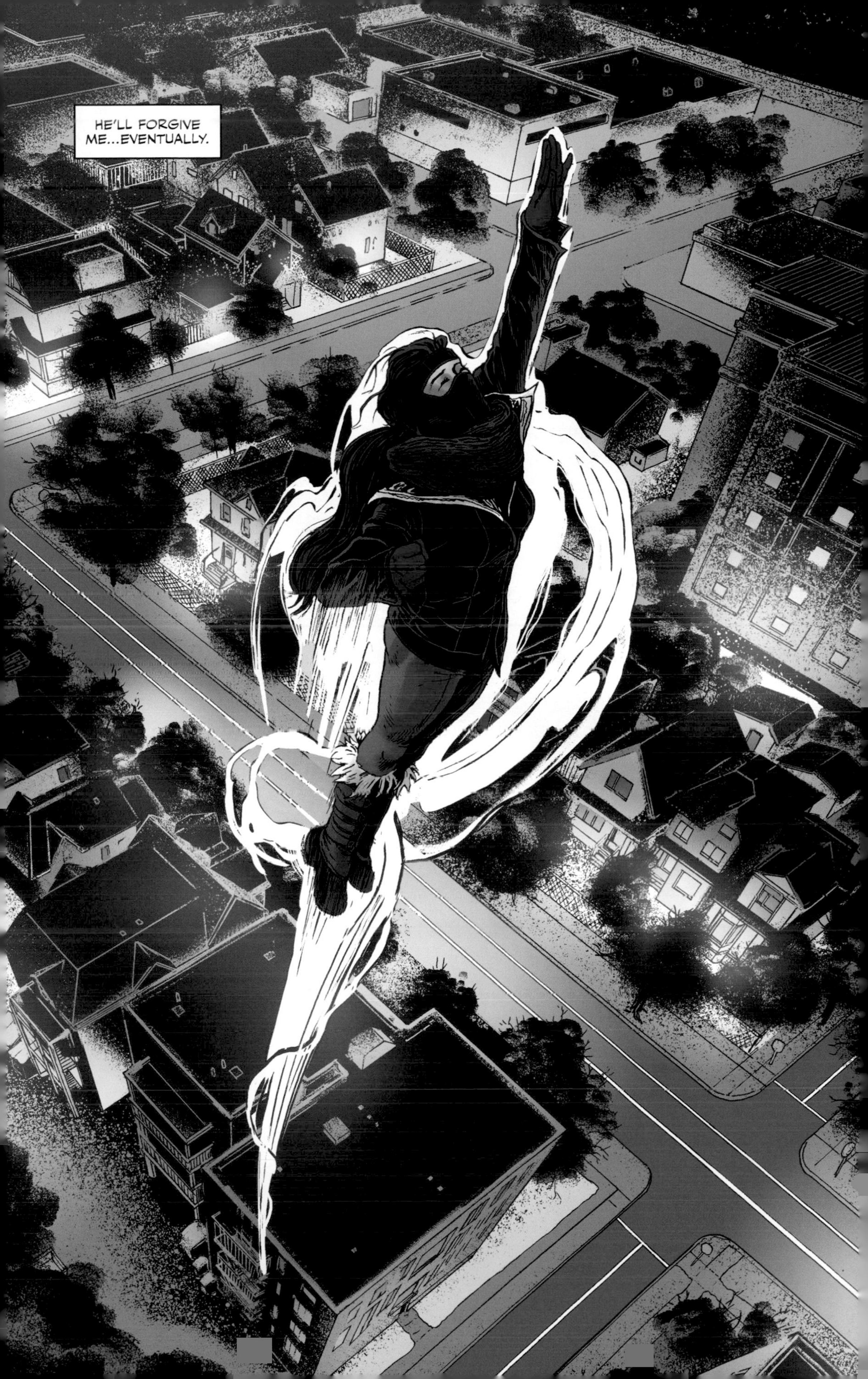
HE'LL FORGIVE ME...EVENTUALLY.

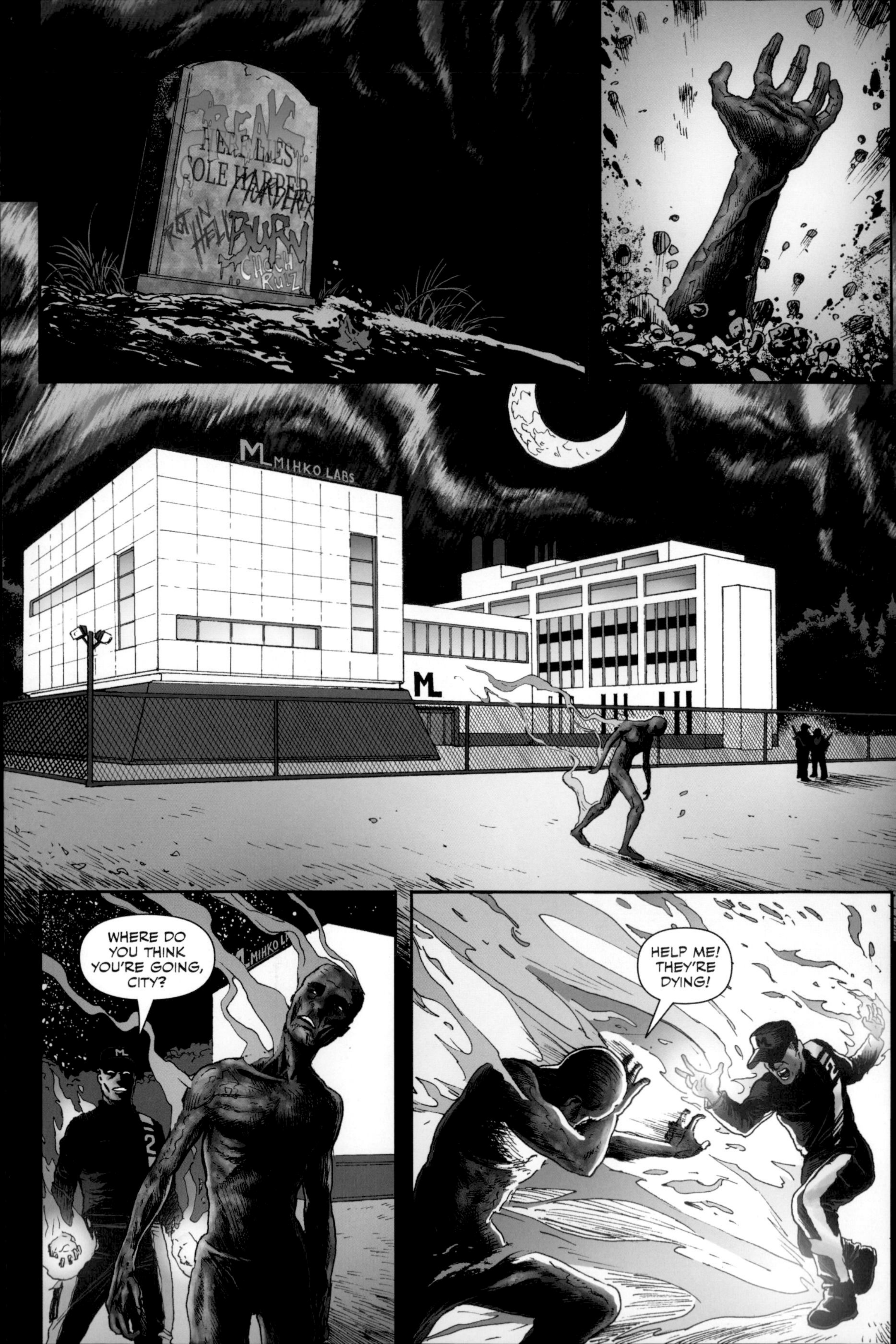
FREAK
HERE LIES
SOLE HARBER
MURDERER
ROT IN HELL
BURN
ML MIHKO LABS
ML
WHERE DO YOU THINK YOU'RE GOING, CITY?
HELP ME! THEY'RE DYING!

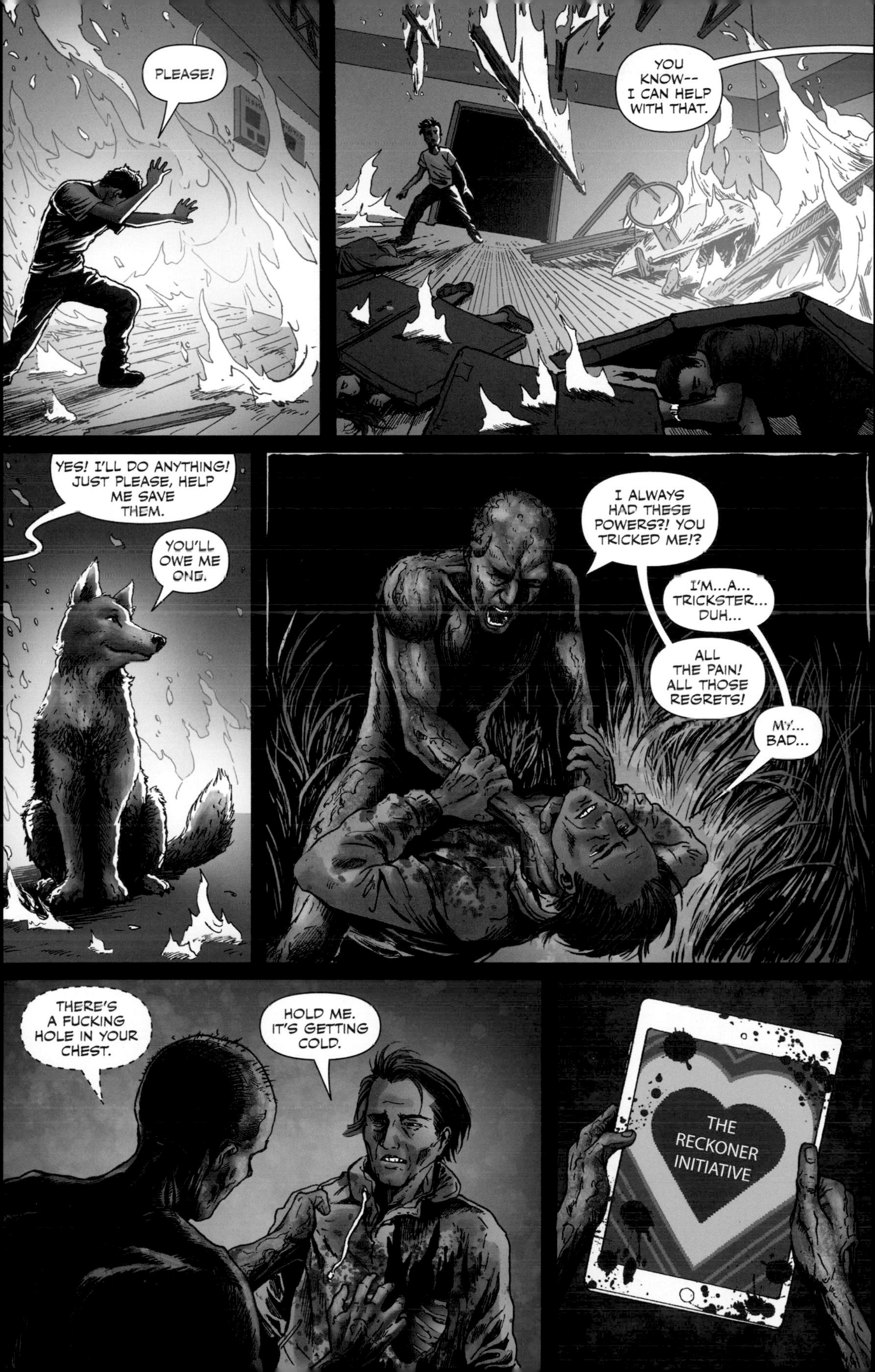
PLEASE!
YOU KNOW-- I CAN HELP WITH THAT.
YES! I'LL DO ANYTHING! JUST PLEASE, HELP ME SAVE THEM.
YOU'LL OWE ME ONE.
I ALWAYS HAD THESE POWERS?! YOU TRICKED ME!?
I'M...A... TRICKSTER... DUH...
ALL THE PAIN! ALL THOSE REGRETS!
MY... BAD...
THERE'S A FUCKING HOLE IN YOUR CHEST.
HOLD ME. IT'S GETTING COLD.
THE RECKONER INITIATIVE

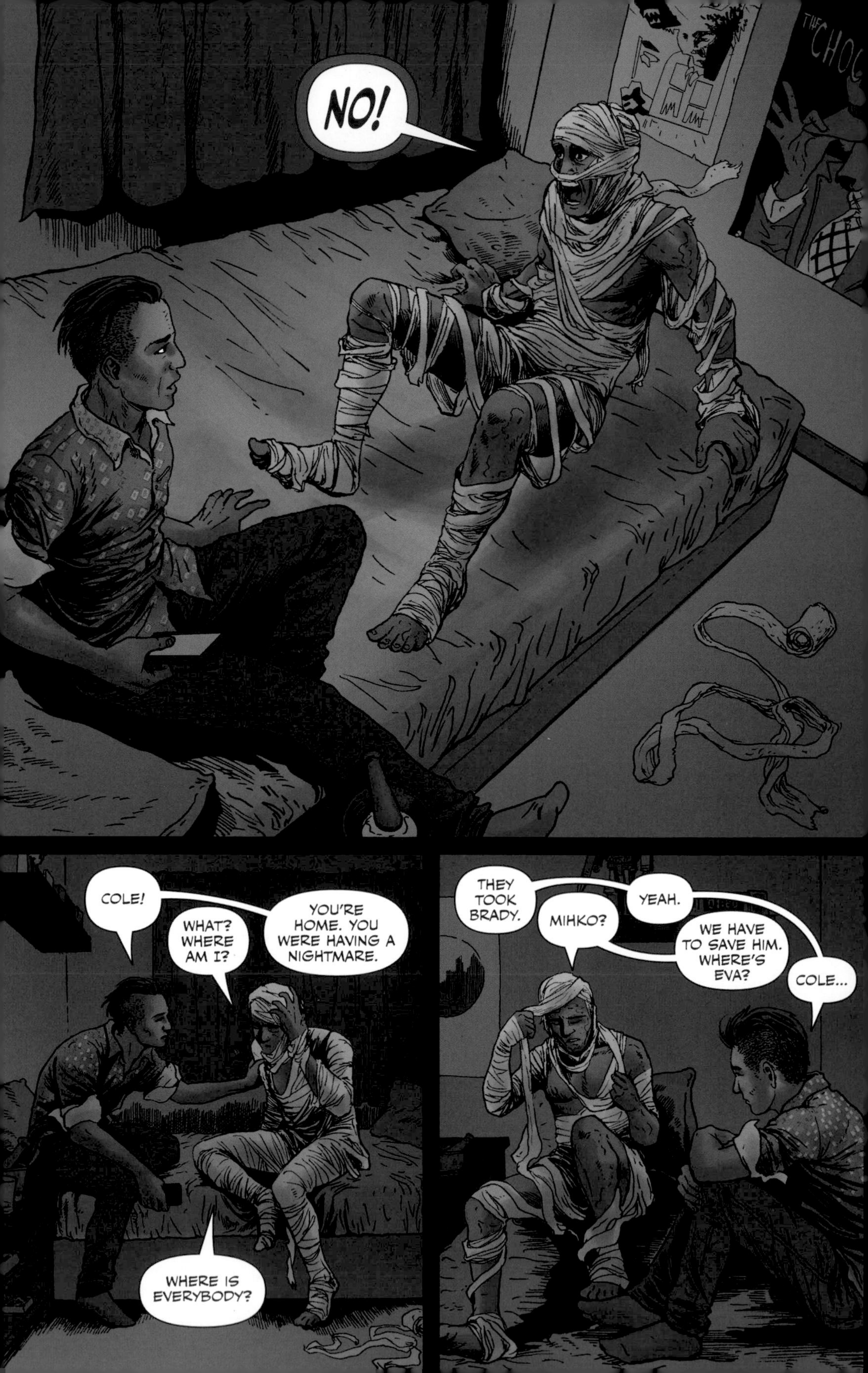
NO!
COLE!
WHAT? WHERE AM I?
YOU'RE HOME. YOU WERE HAVING A NIGHTMARE.
WHERE IS EVERYBODY?
THEY TOOK BRADY.
YEAH.
MIHKO?
WE HAVE TO SAVE HIM. WHERE'S EVA?
COLE...

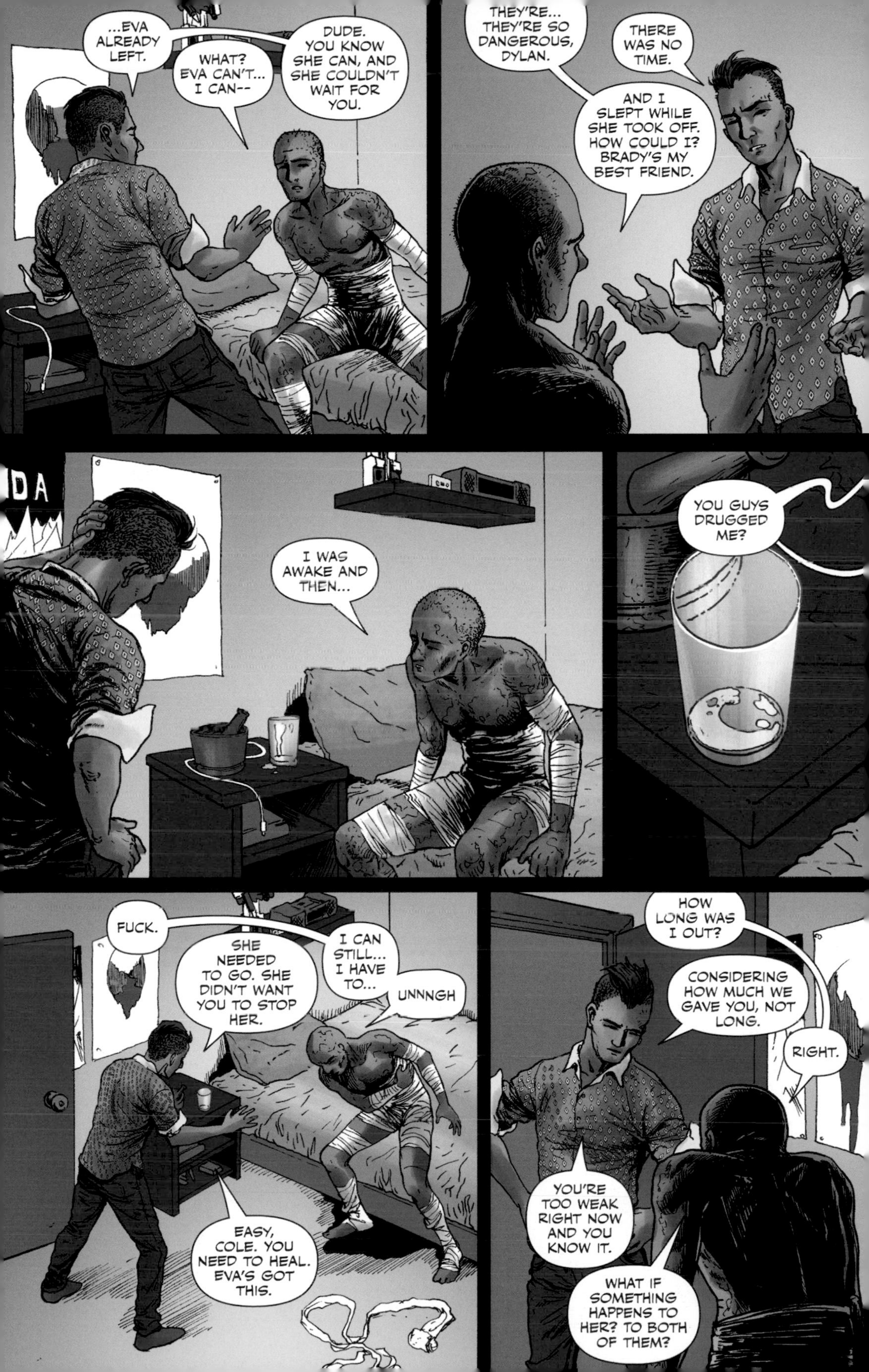
...EVA ALREADY LEFT.
WHAT? EVA CAN'T... I CAN--
DUDE. YOU KNOW SHE CAN, AND SHE COULDN'T WAIT FOR YOU.
THEY'RE... THEY'RE SO DANGEROUS, DYLAN.
THERE WAS NO TIME.
AND I SLEPT WHILE SHE TOOK OFF. HOW COULD I? BRADY'S MY BEST FRIEND.
DA
I WAS AWAKE AND THEN...
YOU GUYS DRUGGED ME?
FUCK.
I CAN STILL... I HAVE TO...
SHE NEEDED TO GO. SHE DIDN'T WANT YOU TO STOP HER.
UNNNGH
EASY, COLE. YOU NEED TO HEAL. EVA'S GOT THIS.
HOW LONG WAS I OUT?
CONSIDERING HOW MUCH WE GAVE YOU, NOT LONG.
RIGHT.
YOU'RE TOO WEAK RIGHT NOW AND YOU KNOW IT.
WHAT IF SOMETHING HAPPENS TO HER? TO BOTH OF THEM?

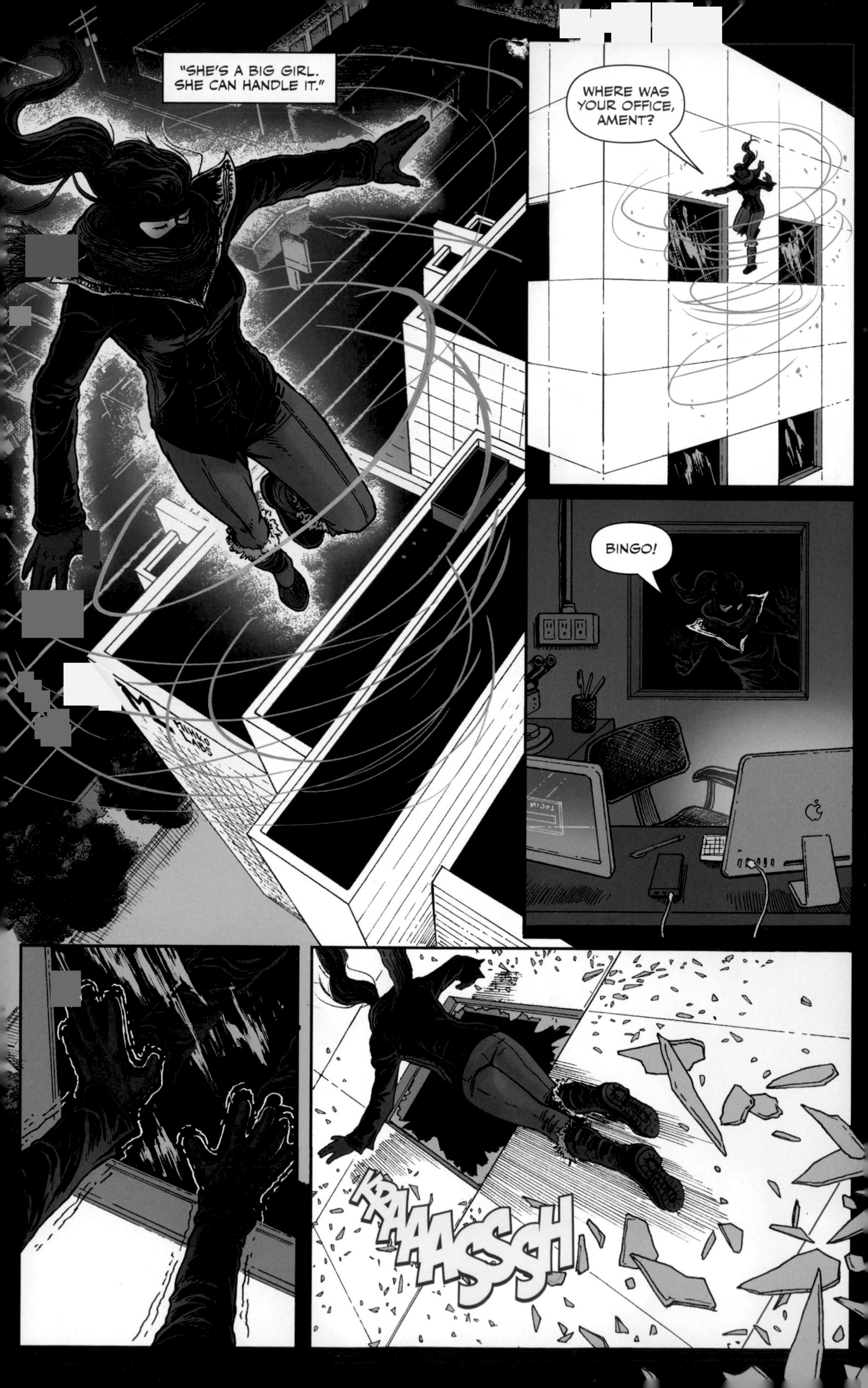
"SHE'S A BIG GIRL. SHE CAN HANDLE IT."
WHERE WAS YOUR OFFICE, AMENT?
BINGO!
KRAAASSGH

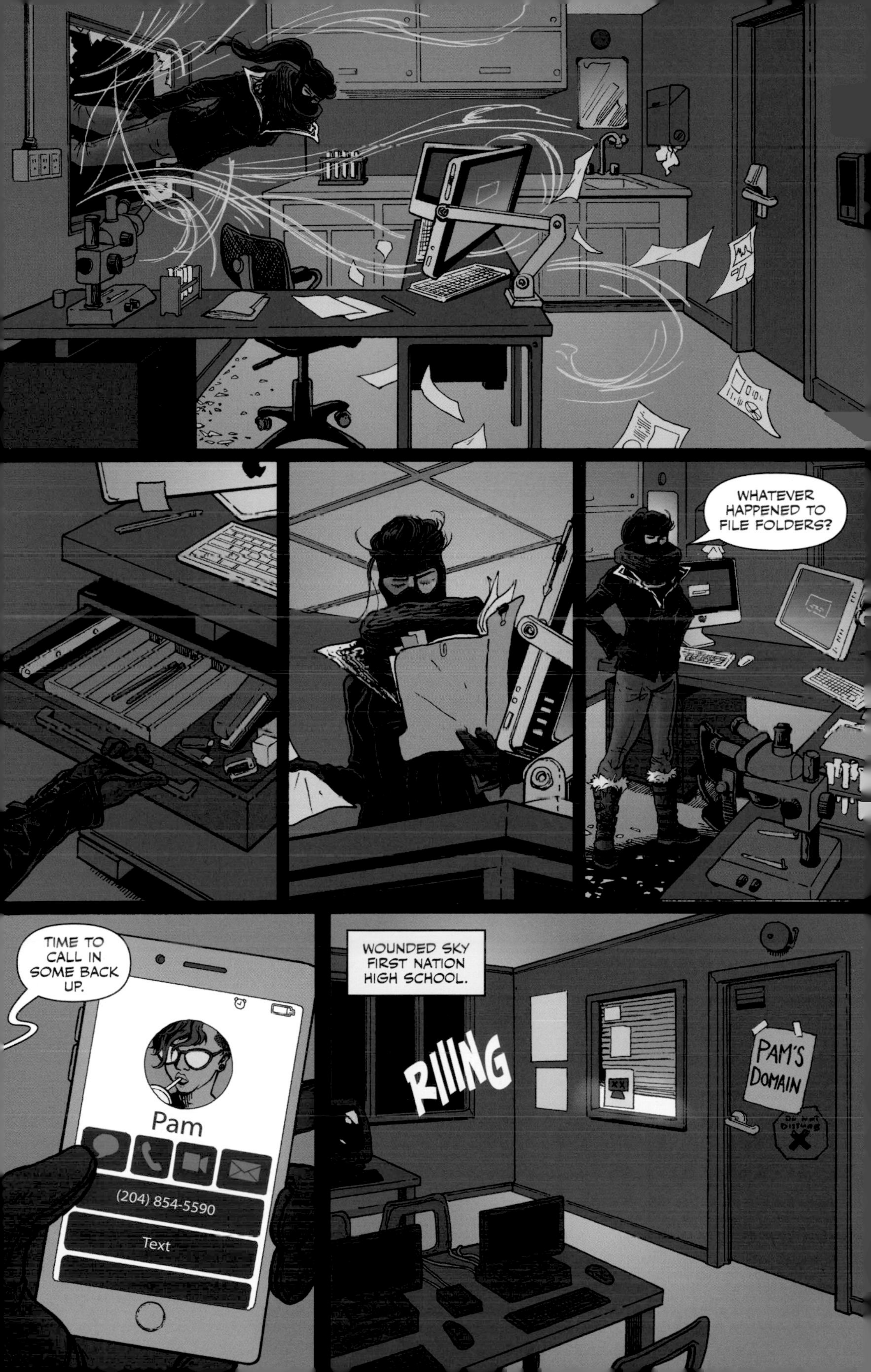
WHATEVER HAPPENED TO FILE FOLDERS?
TIME TO CALL IN SOME BACK UP.
Pam
(204) 854-5590
Text
WOUNDED SKY FIRST NATION HIGH SCHOOL.
RIIING
PAM'S DOMAIN

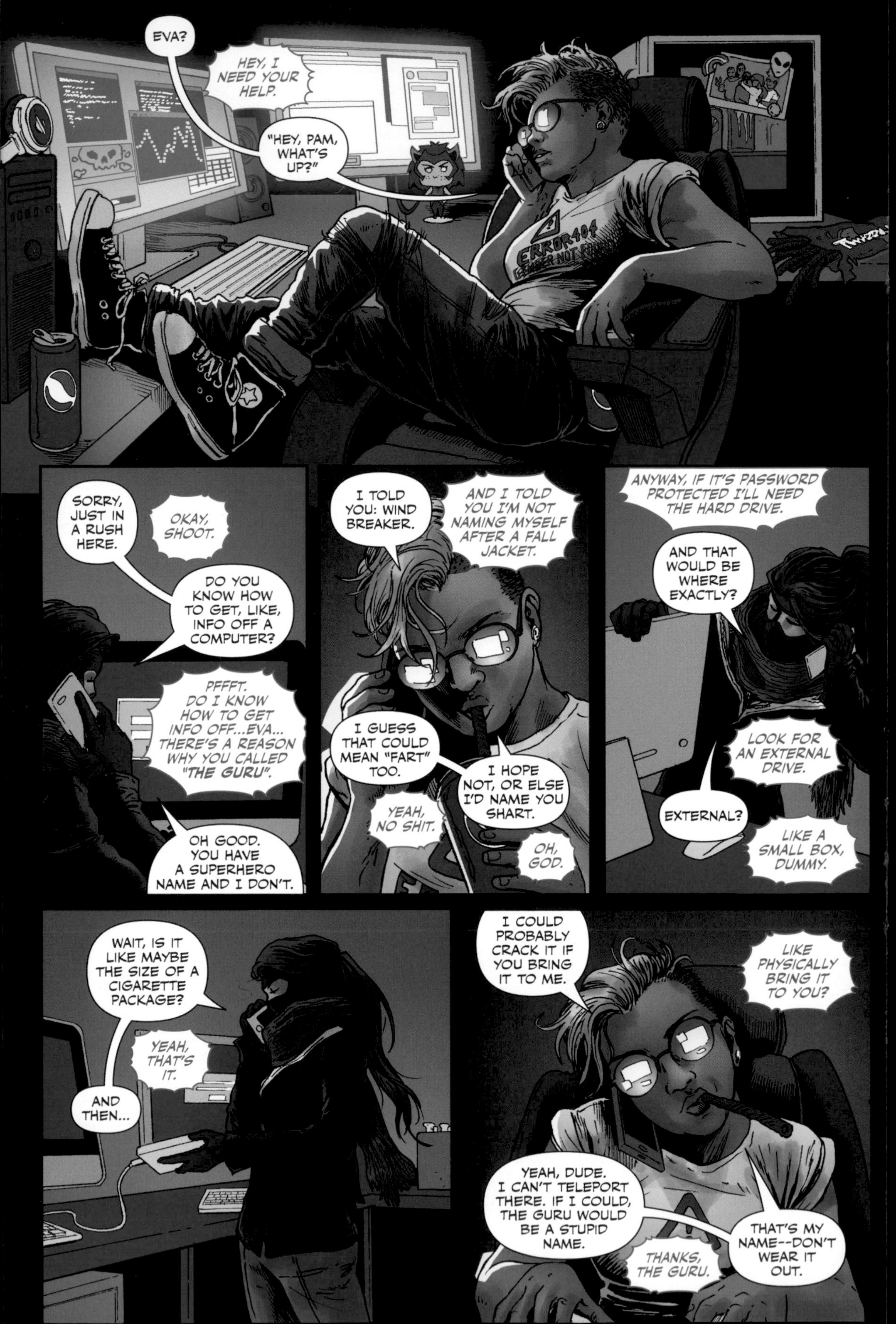

EVA?
HEY, I NEED YOUR HELP.
"HEY, PAM, WHAT'S UP?"
ERROR 404
SORRY, JUST IN A RUSH HERE.
OKAY, SHOOT.
DO YOU KNOW HOW TO GET, LIKE, INFO OFF A COMPUTER?
PFFFT. DO I KNOW HOW TO GET INFO OFF...EVA... THERE'S A REASON WHY YOU CALLED "THE GURU".
OH GOOD. YOU HAVE A SUPERHERO NAME AND I DON'T.
I TOLD YOU: WIND BREAKER.
AND I TOLD YOU I'M NOT NAMING MYSELF AFTER A FALL JACKET.
I GUESS THAT COULD MEAN "FART" TOO.
I HOPE NOT, OR ELSE I'D NAME YOU SHART.
YEAH, NO SHIT.
OH, GOD.
ANYWAY, IF IT'S PASSWORD PROTECTED I'LL NEED THE HARD DRIVE.
AND THAT WOULD BE WHERE EXACTLY?
LOOK FOR AN EXTERNAL DRIVE.
EXTERNAL?
LIKE A SMALL BOX, DUMMY.
WAIT, IS IT LIKE MAYBE THE SIZE OF A CIGARETTE PACKAGE?
YEAH, THAT'S IT.
AND THEN...
I COULD PROBABLY CRACK IT IF YOU BRING IT TO ME.
LIKE PHYSICALLY BRING IT TO YOU?
YEAH, DUDE. I CAN'T TELEPORT THERE. IF I COULD, THE GURU WOULD BE A STUPID NAME.
THANKS, THE GURU.
THAT'S MY NAME--DON'T WEAR IT OUT.

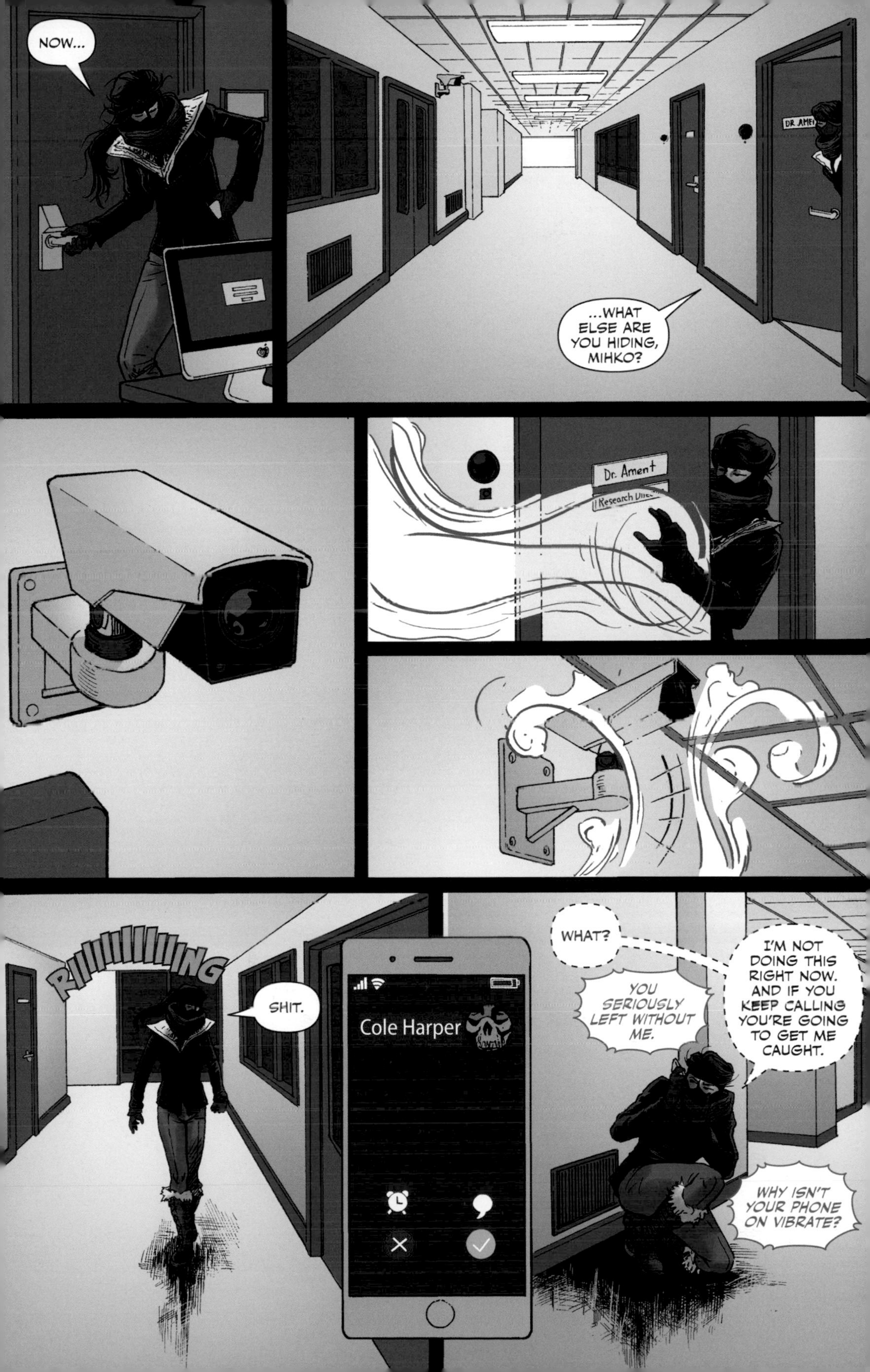
NOW...
...WHAT ELSE ARE YOU HIDING, MIHKO?
DR. AMEN
Dr. Ament
Research Direc
RIIIIIIIIIING
SHIT.
Cole Harper
WHAT?
YOU SERIOUSLY LEFT WITHOUT ME.
I'M NOT DOING THIS RIGHT NOW. AND IF YOU KEEP CALLING YOU'RE GOING TO GET ME CAUGHT.
WHY ISN'T YOUR PHONE ON VIBRATE?

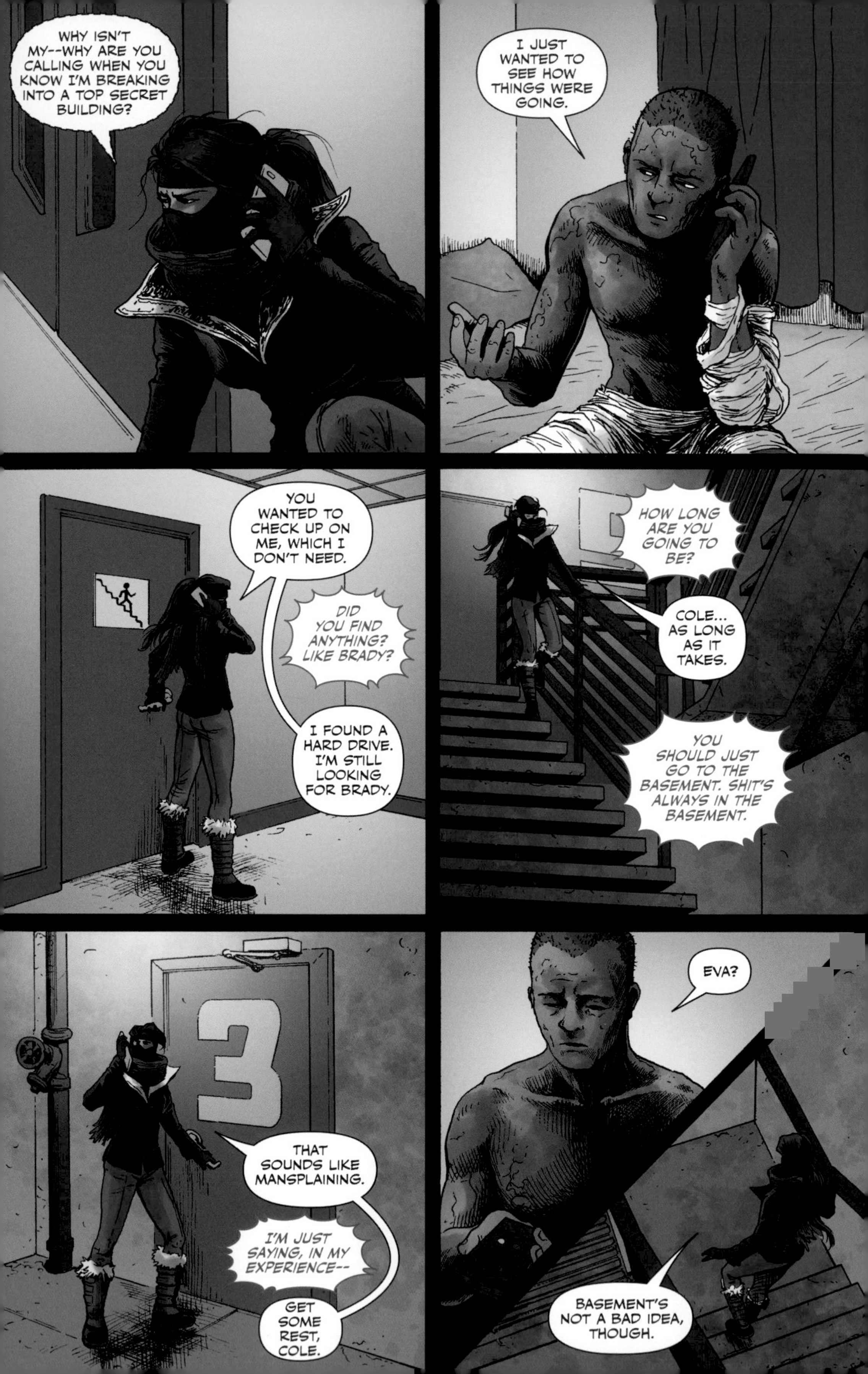
WHY ISN'T MY--WHY ARE YOU CALLING WHEN YOU KNOW I'M BREAKING INTO A TOP SECRET BUILDING?
I JUST WANTED TO SEE HOW THINGS WERE GOING.
YOU WANTED TO CHECK UP ON ME, WHICH I DON'T NEED.
DID YOU FIND ANYTHING? LIKE BRADY?
I FOUND A HARD DRIVE. I'M STILL LOOKING FOR BRADY.
HOW LONG ARE YOU GOING TO BE?
COLE... AS LONG AS IT TAKES.
YOU SHOULD JUST GO TO THE BASEMENT. SHIT'S ALWAYS IN THE BASEMENT.
3
THAT SOUNDS LIKE MANSPLAINING.
I'M JUST SAYING, IN MY EXPERIENCE--
GET SOME REST, COLE.
EVA?
BASEMENT'S NOT A BAD IDEA, THOUGH.

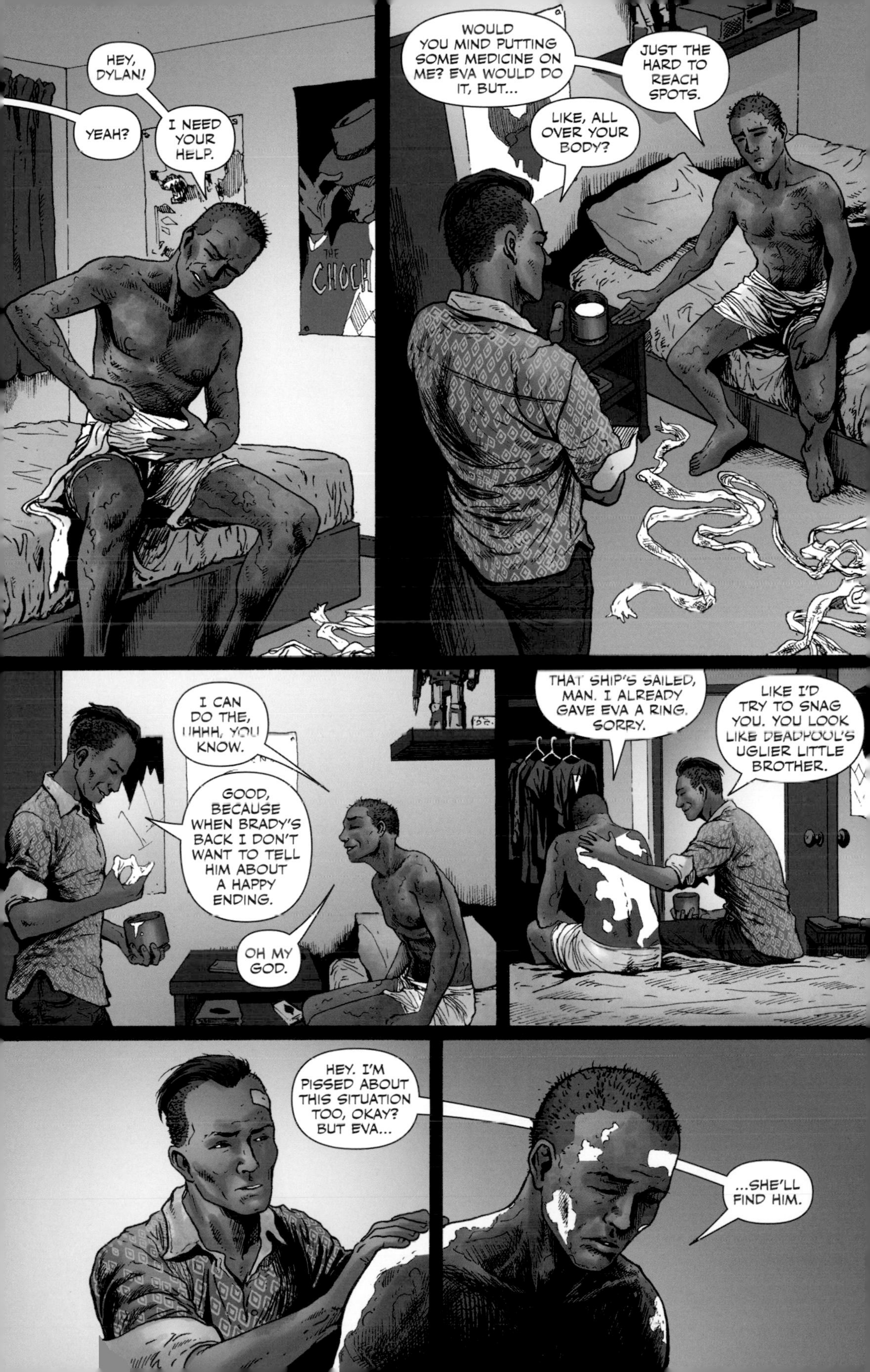
HEY, DYLAN!
YEAH?
I NEED YOUR HELP.
WOULD YOU MIND PUTTING SOME MEDICINE ON ME? EVA WOULD DO IT, BUT...
JUST THE HARD TO REACH SPOTS.
LIKE, ALL OVER YOUR BODY?
THE CHOCH
I CAN DO THE, UHHH, YOU KNOW.
GOOD, BECAUSE WHEN BRADY'S BACK I DON'T WANT TO TELL HIM ABOUT A HAPPY ENDING.
OH MY GOD.
THAT SHIP'S SAILED, MAN. I ALREADY GAVE EVA A RING. SORRY.
LIKE I'D TRY TO SNAG YOU. YOU LOOK LIKE DEADPOOL'S UGLIER LITTLE BROTHER.
HEY. I'M PISSED ABOUT THIS SITUATION TOO, OKAY? BUT EVA...
...SHE'LL FIND HIM.

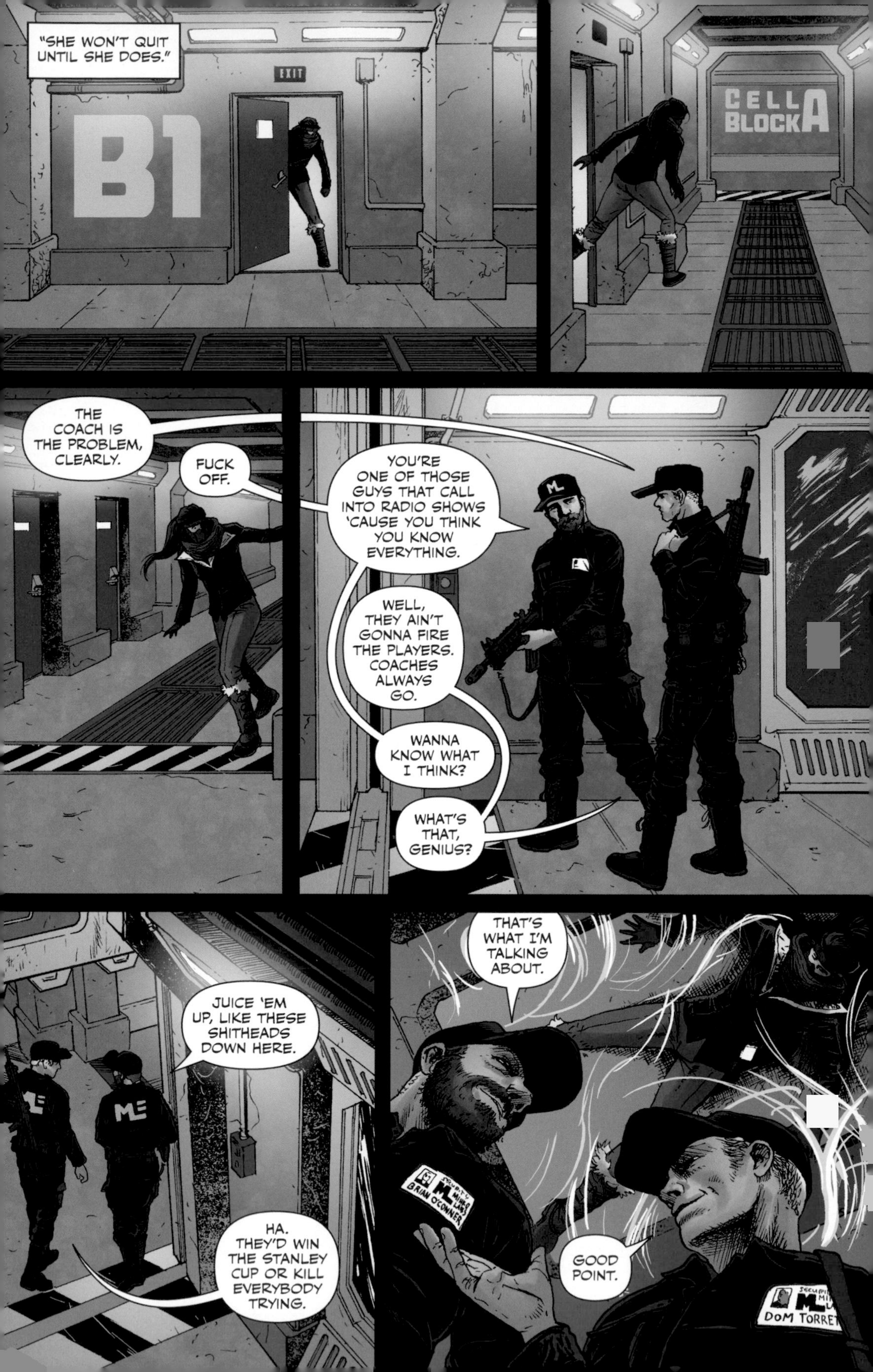
"SHE WON'T QUIT UNTIL SHE DOES."
EXIT
B1
CELL BLOCK A
THE COACH IS THE PROBLEM, CLEARLY.
FUCK OFF.
YOU'RE ONE OF THOSE GUYS THAT CALL INTO RADIO SHOWS 'CAUSE YOU THINK YOU KNOW EVERYTHING.
WELL, THEY AIN'T GONNA FIRE THE PLAYERS. COACHES ALWAYS GO.
WANNA KNOW WHAT I THINK?
WHAT'S THAT, GENIUS?
JUICE 'EM UP, LIKE THESE SHITHEADS DOWN HERE.
HA. THEY'D WIN THE STANLEY CUP OR KILL EVERYBODY TRYING.
THAT'S WHAT I'M TALKING ABOUT.
BRIAN O'CONNER
GOOD POINT.
DOM TORRET

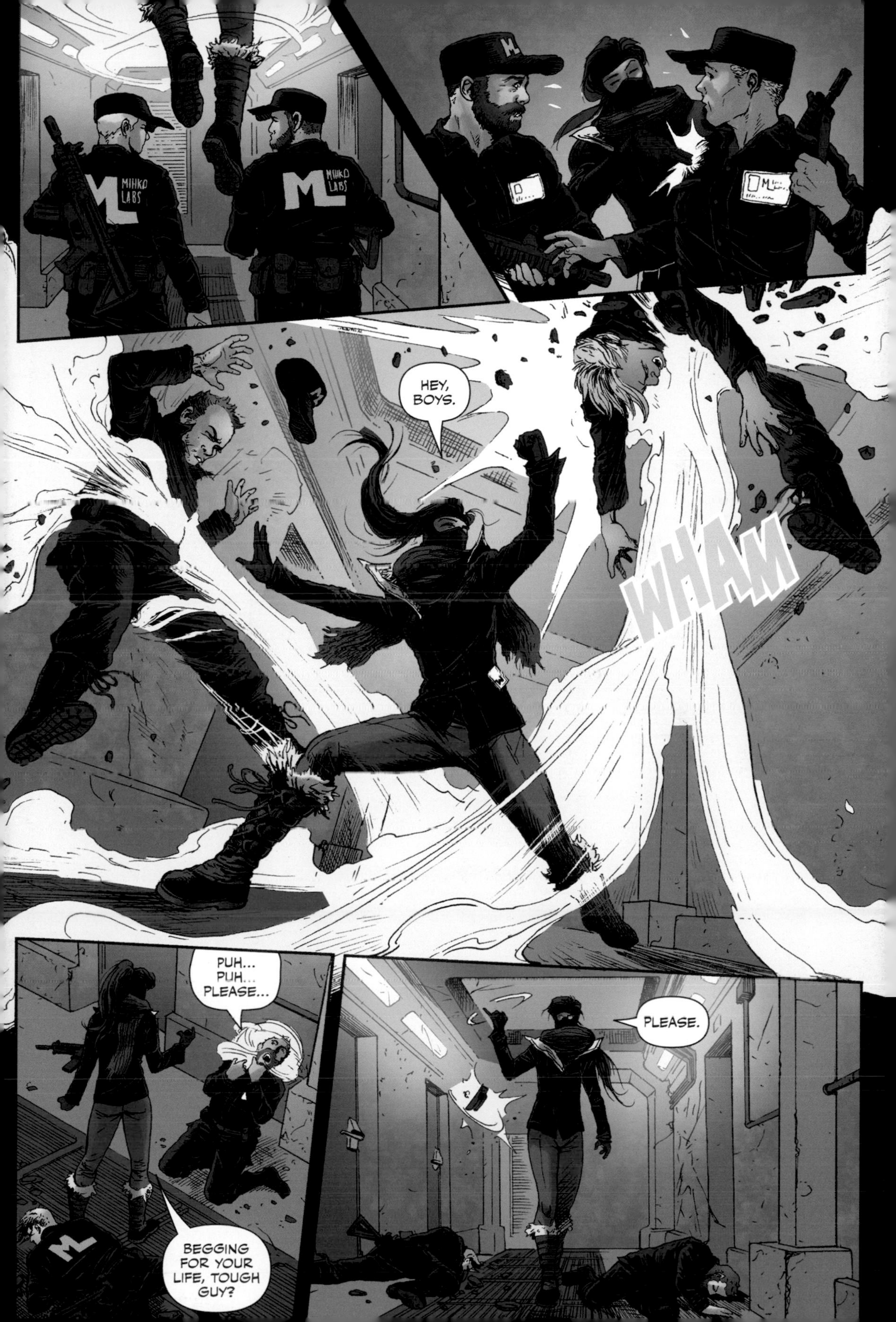
MIHKO LABS
HEY, BOYS.
WHAM
PUH... PUH... PLEASE...
BEGGING FOR YOUR LIFE, TOUGH GUY?
PLEASE.

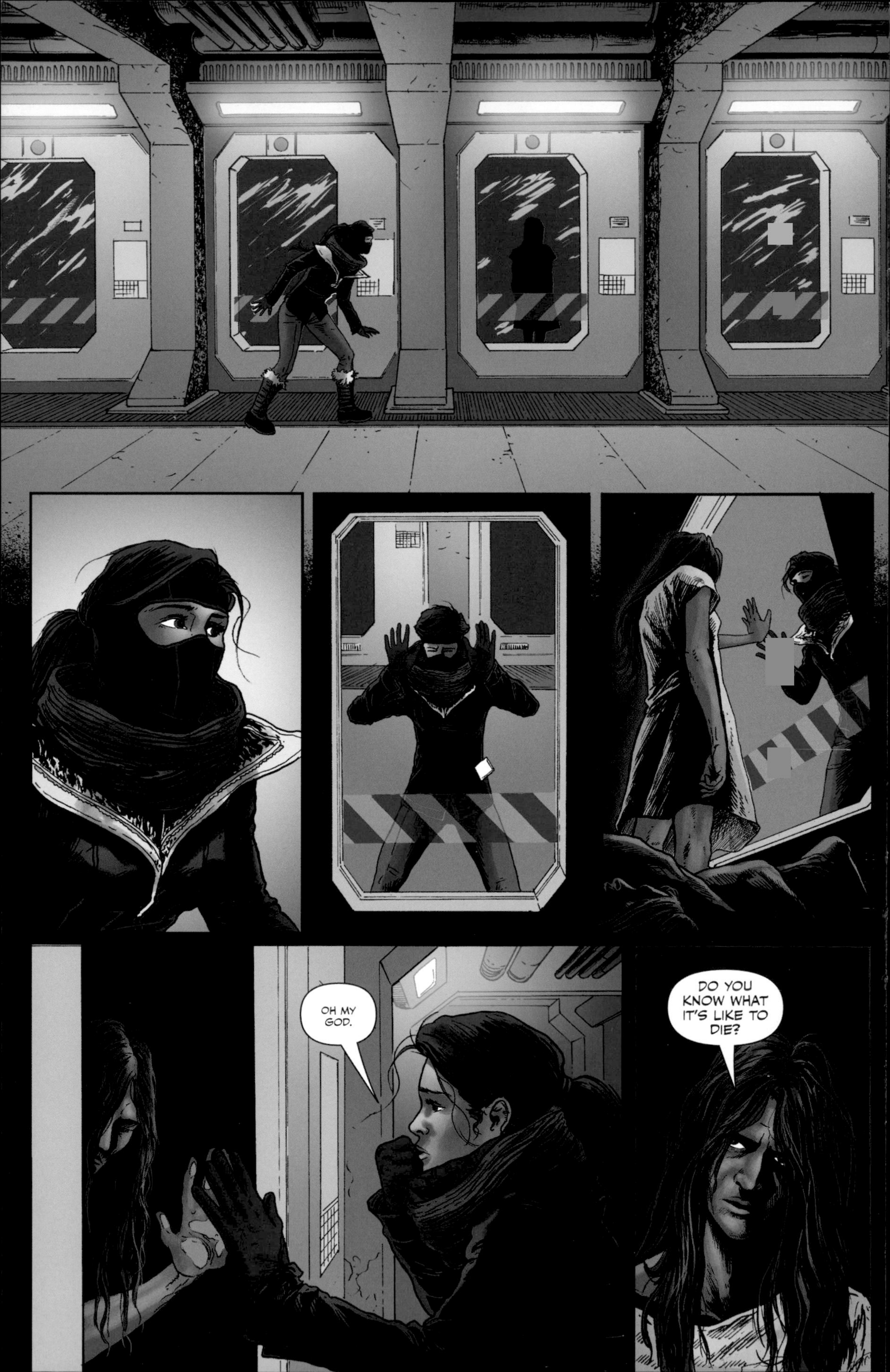
OH MY GOD.
DO YOU KNOW WHAT IT'S LIKE TO DIE?

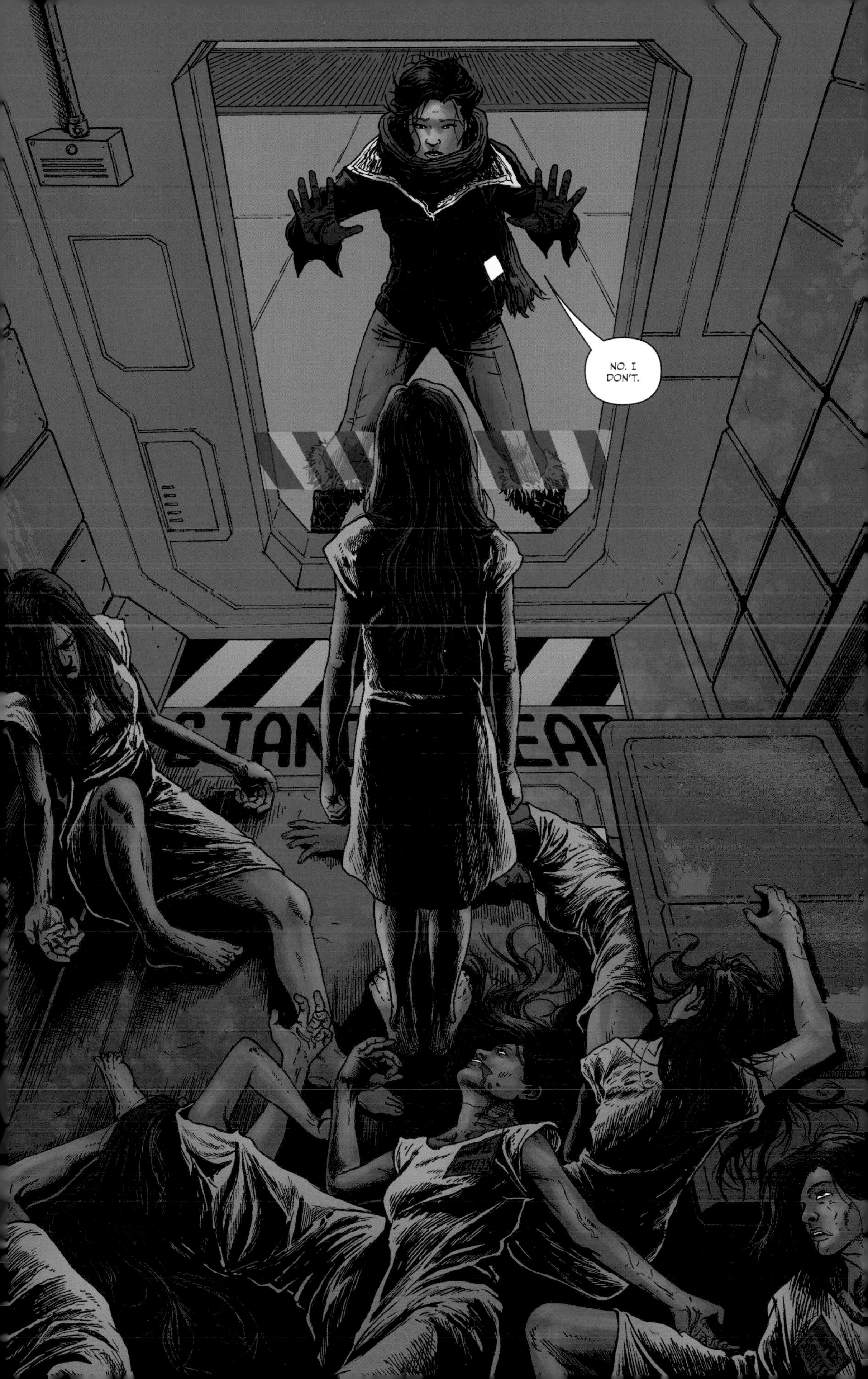
NO. I DON'T.

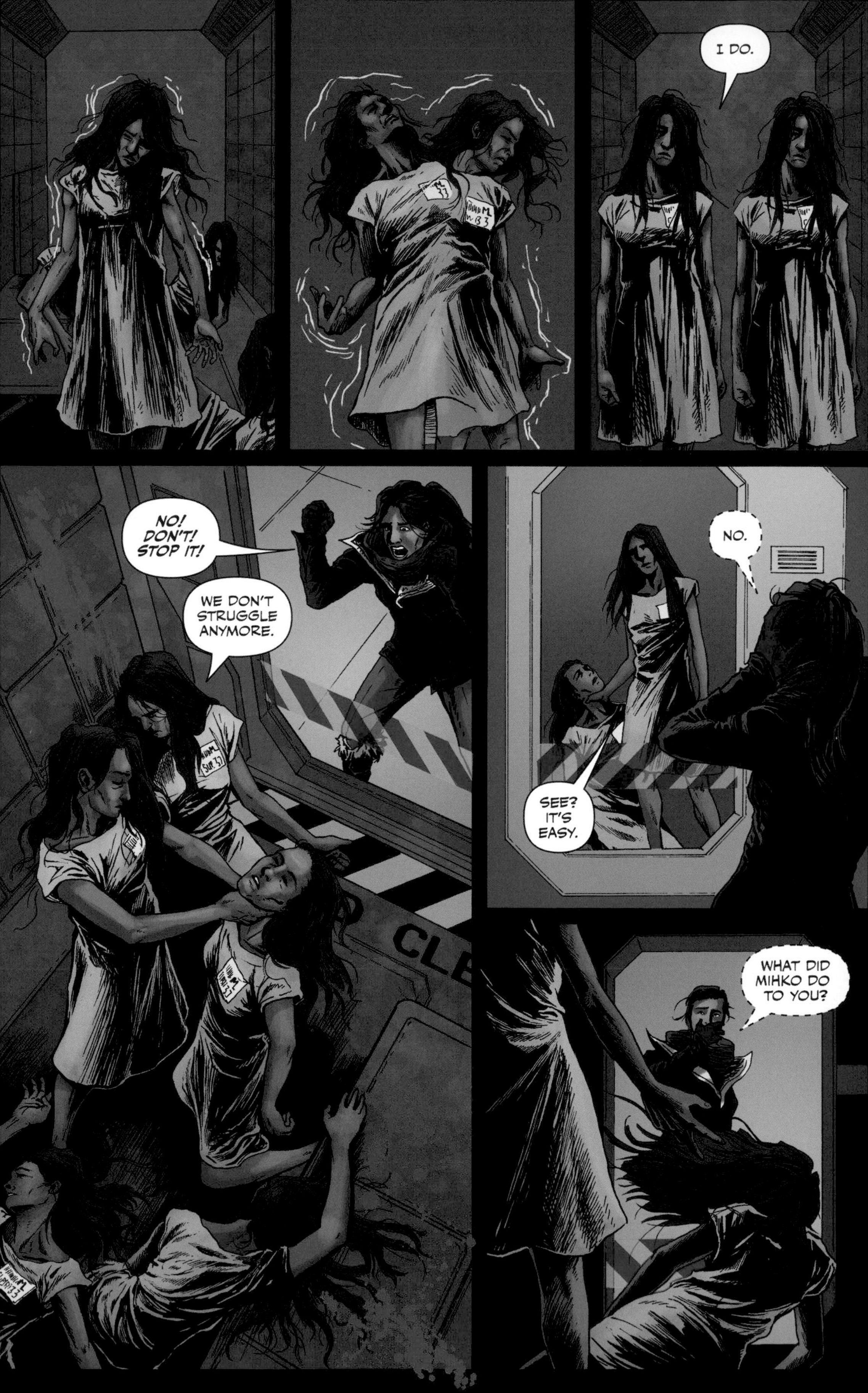
I DO.
NO! DON'T! STOP IT!
WE DON'T STRUGGLE ANYMORE.
CLE
NO.
SEE? IT'S EASY.
WHAT DID MIHKO DO TO YOU?

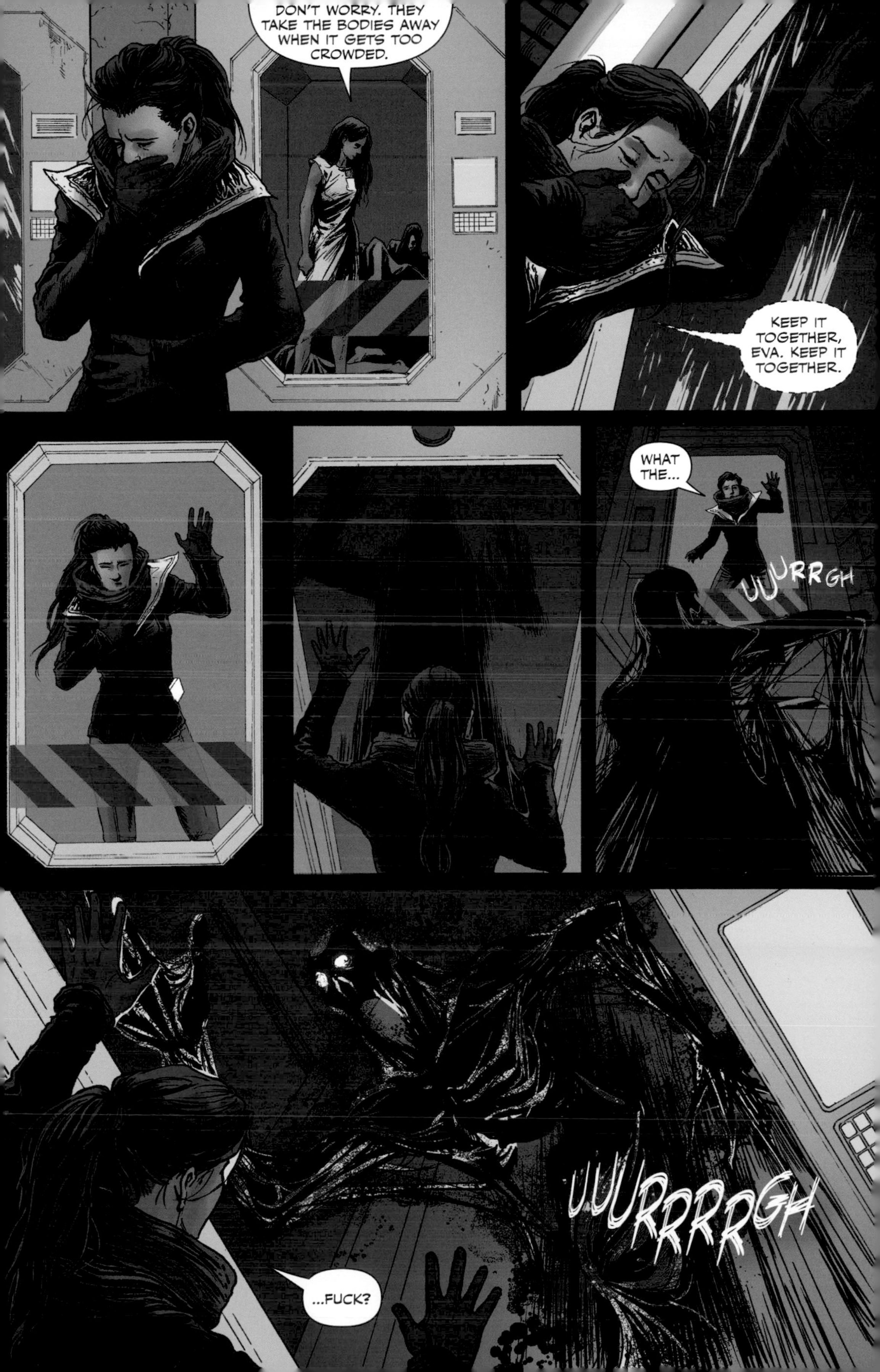
DON'T WORRY. THEY TAKE THE BODIES AWAY WHEN IT GETS TOO CROWDED.
KEEP IT TOGETHER, EVA. KEEP IT TOGETHER.
WHAT THE...
UURRGH
UUURRRRGH
...FUCK?

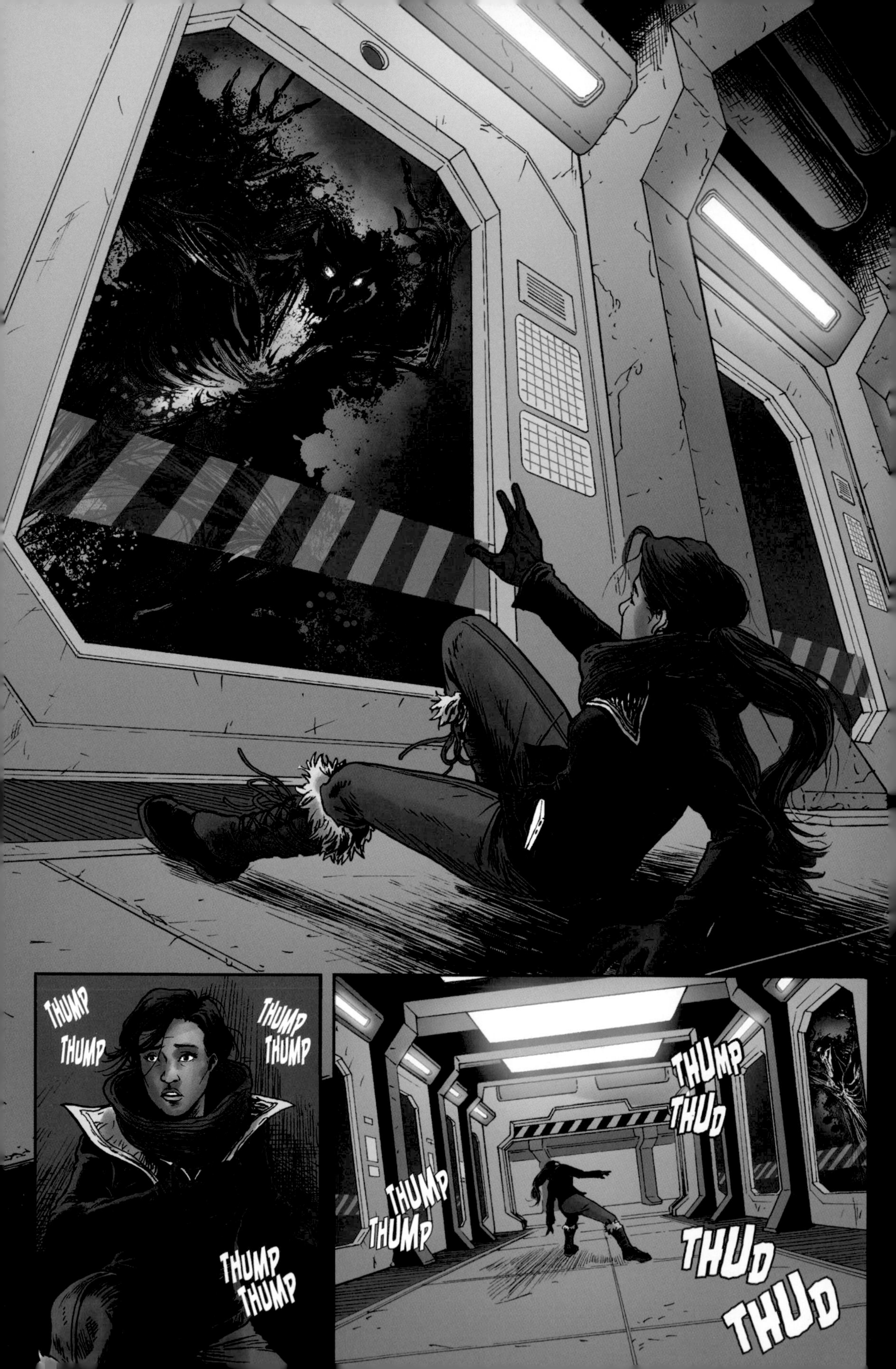
THUMP
THUMP
THUMP
THUMP
THUMP
THUMP
THUMP
THUD
THUMP
THUMP
THUD
THUD

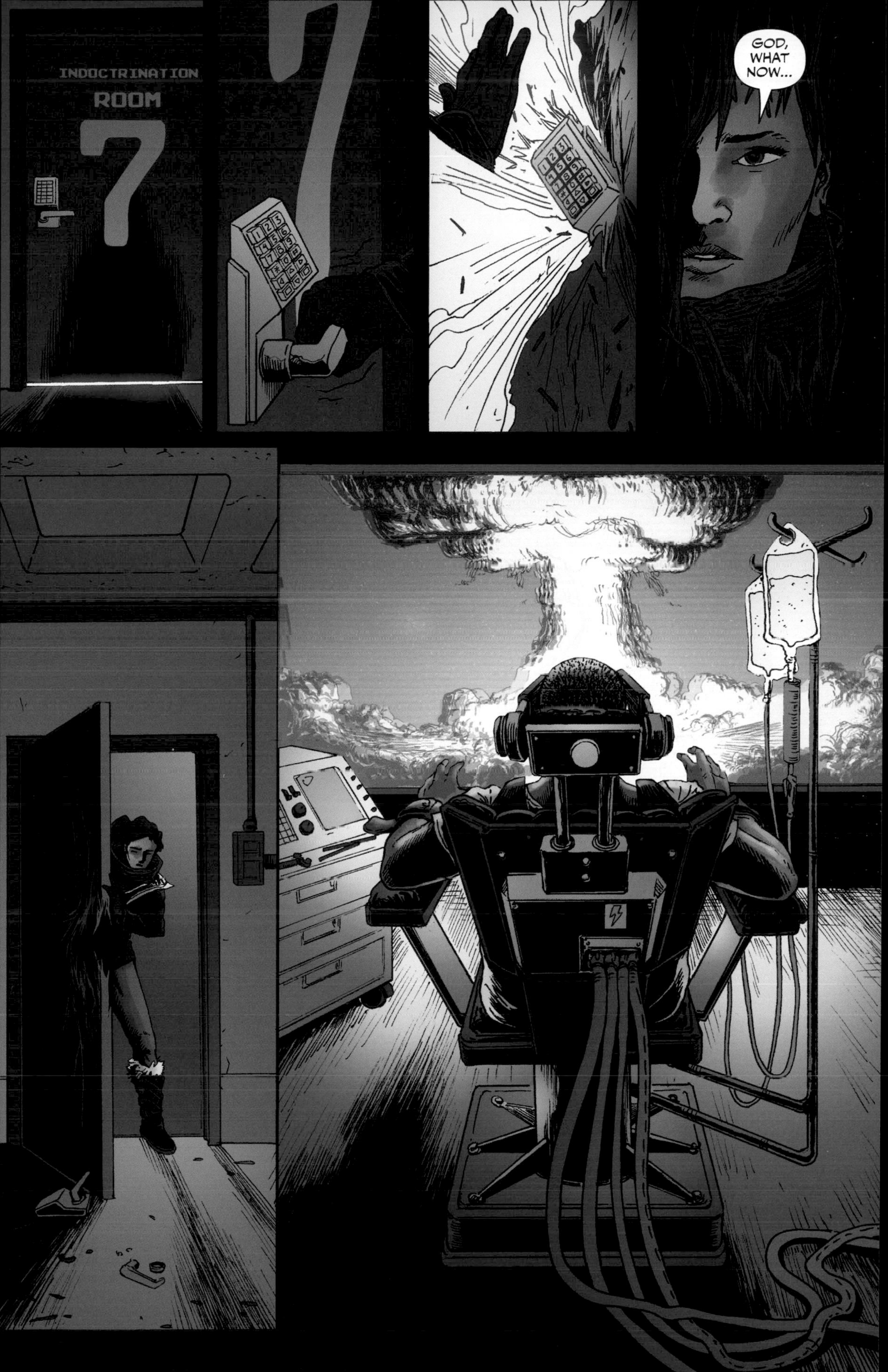
INDOCTRINATION
ROOM
7
GOD, WHAT NOW...

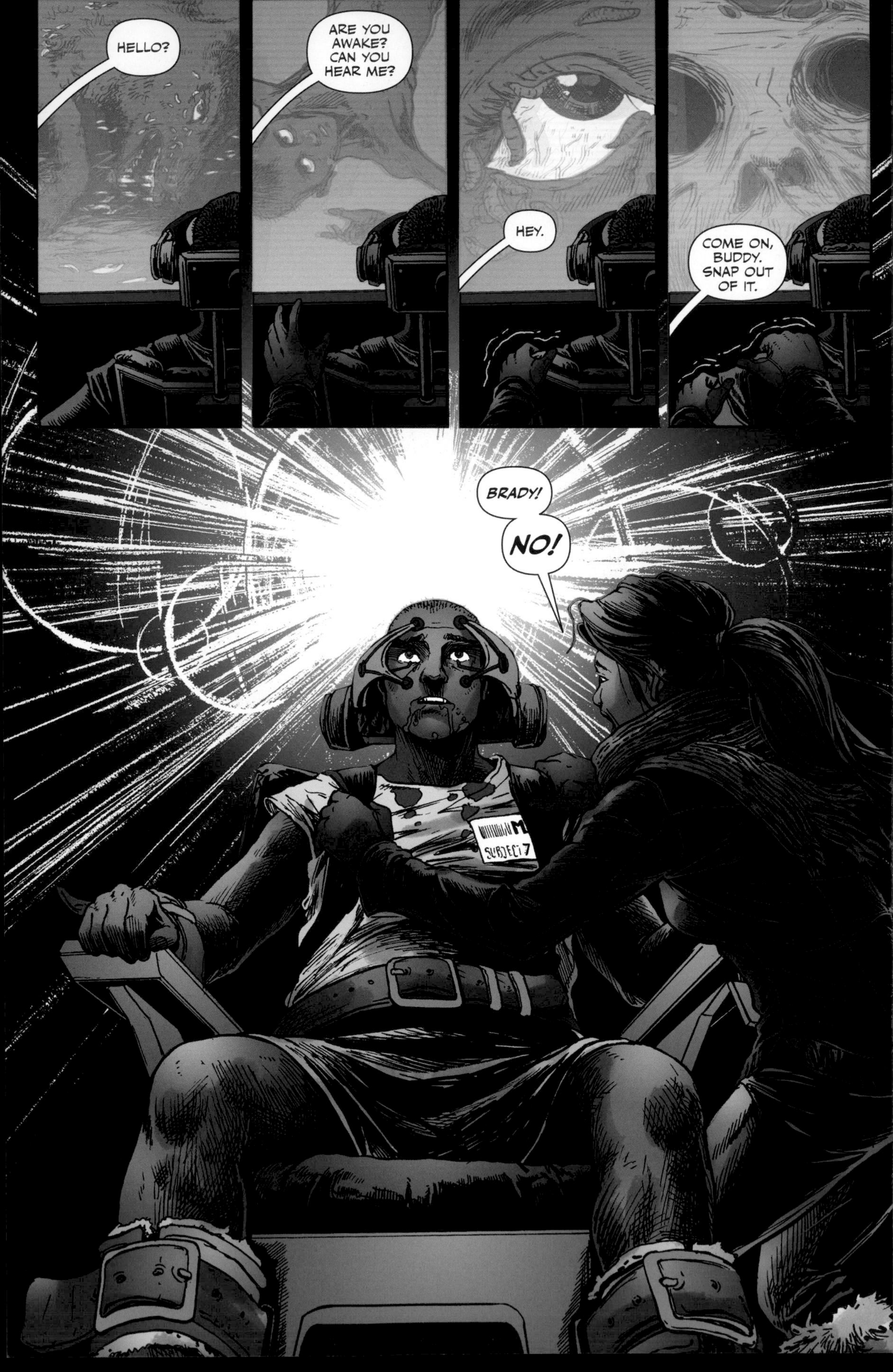
HELLO?
ARE YOU AWAKE? CAN YOU HEAR ME?
HEY.
COME ON, BUDDY. SNAP OUT OF IT.
BRADY!
NO!
SUBJECT 7

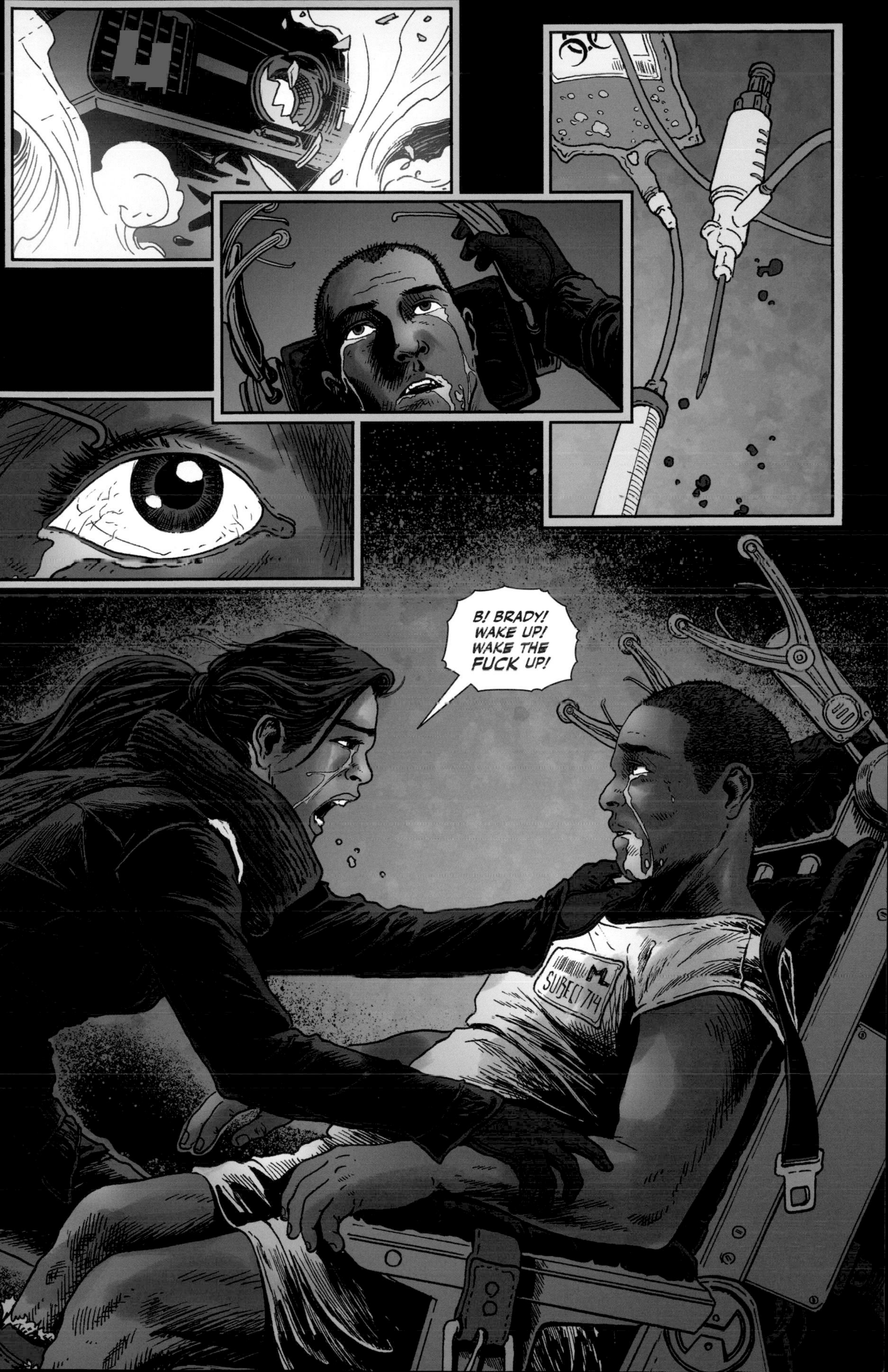
B! BRADY! WAKE UP! WAKE THE FUCK UP!
SUBJECT 714

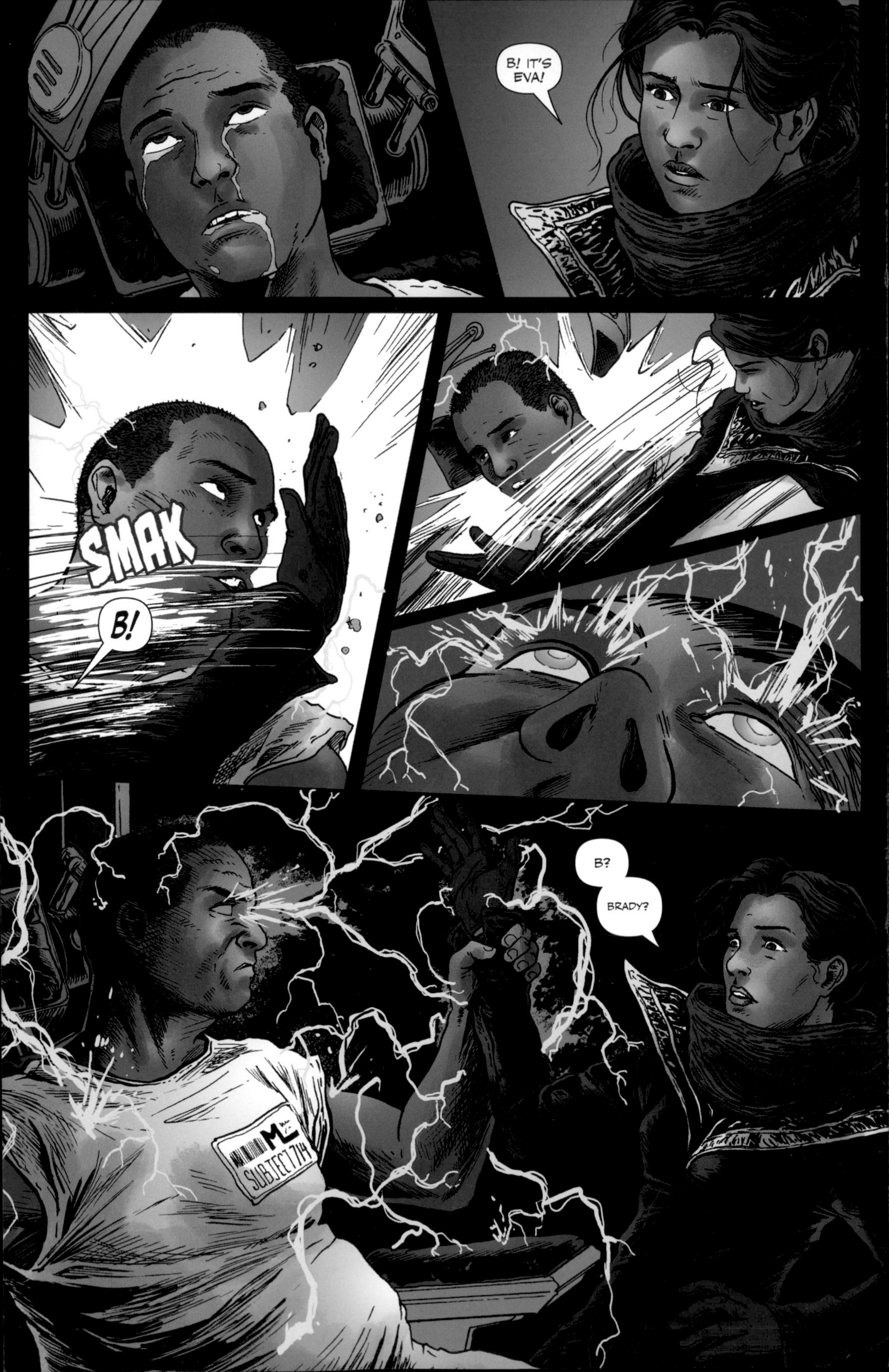
B! IT'S EVA!
SMAK
B!
B?
BRADY?
SUBJECT 714

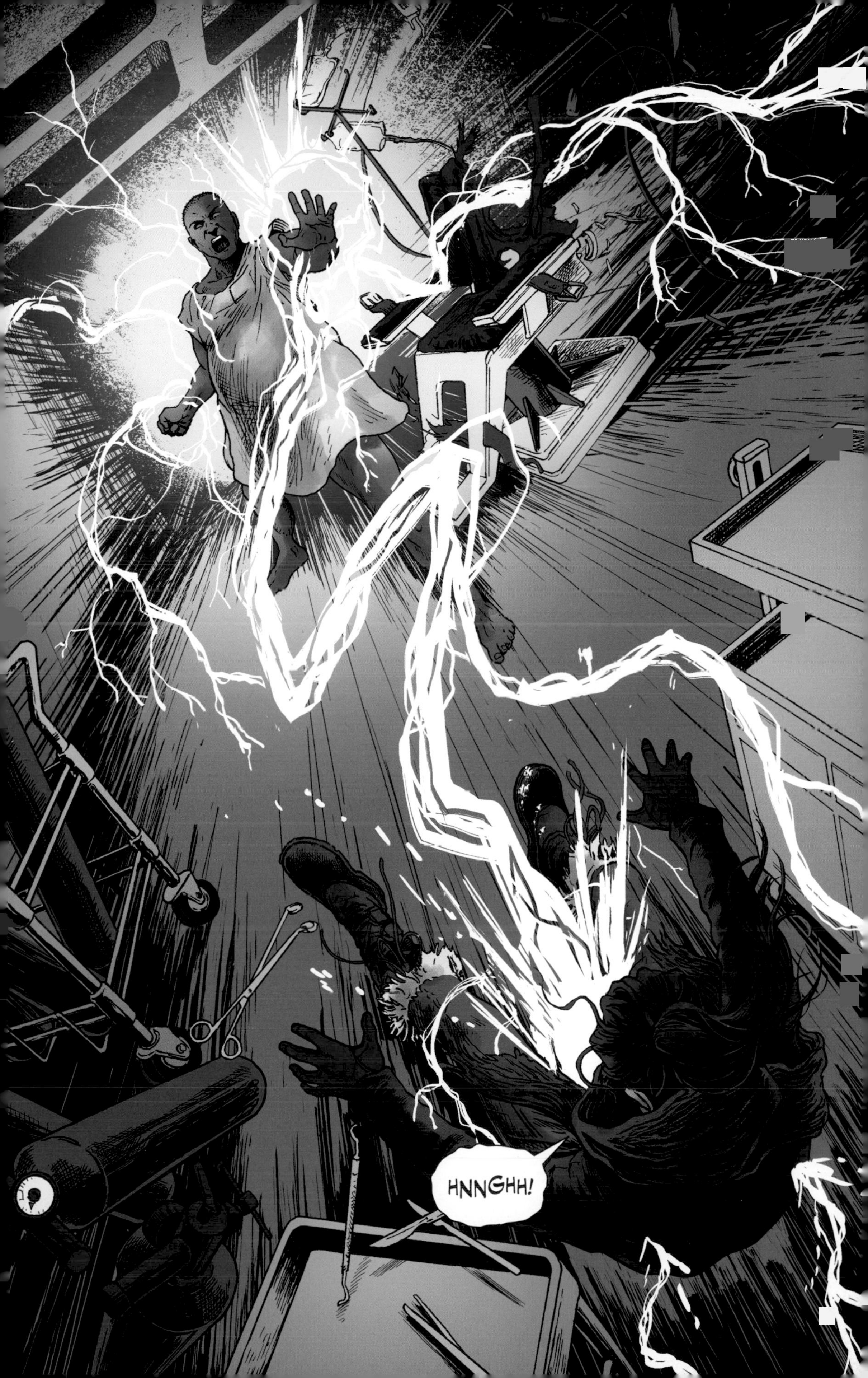
HNNGHH!

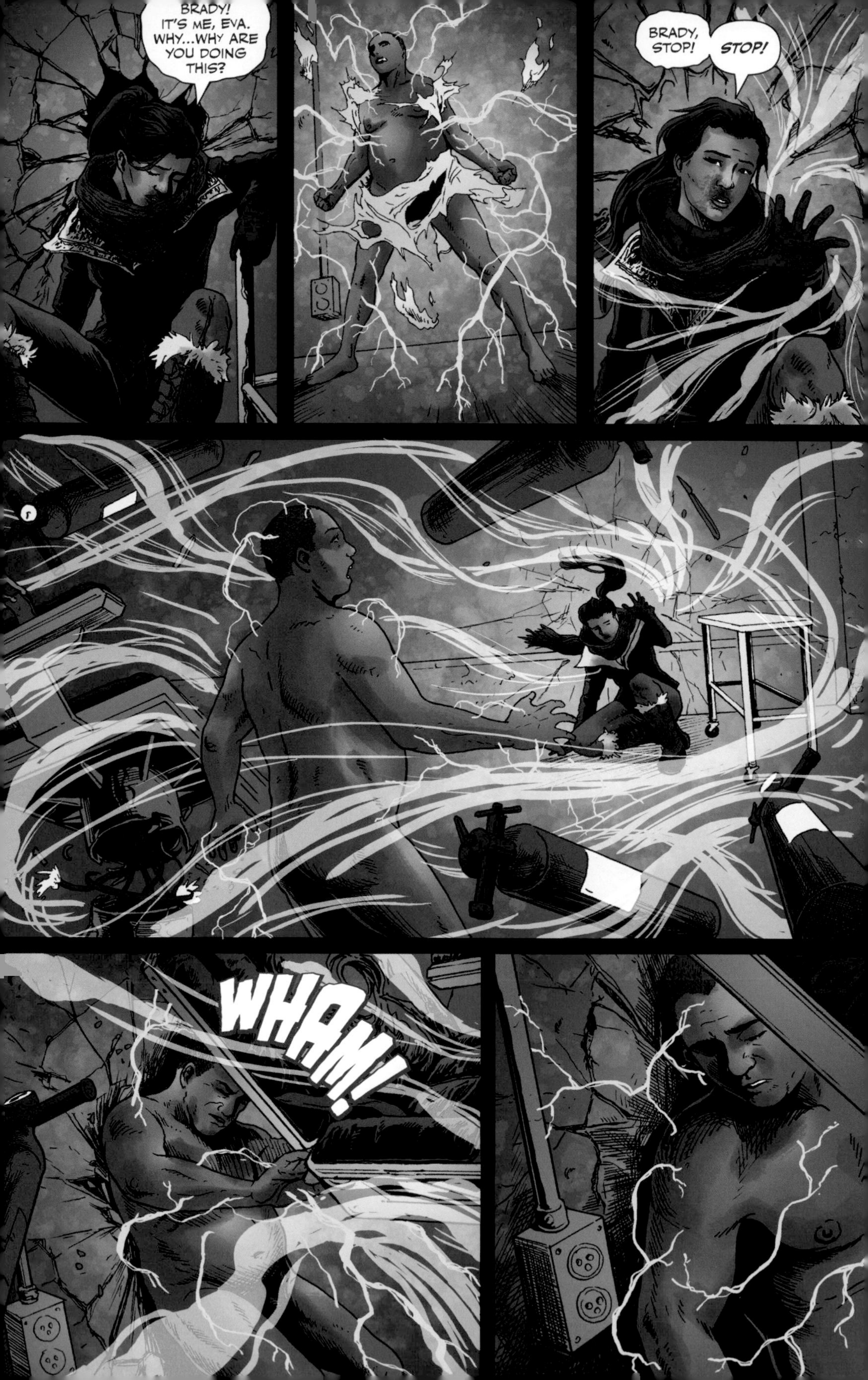
BRADY! IT'S ME, EVA. WHY...WHY ARE YOU DOING THIS?
BRADY, STOP!
STOP!
WHAM!

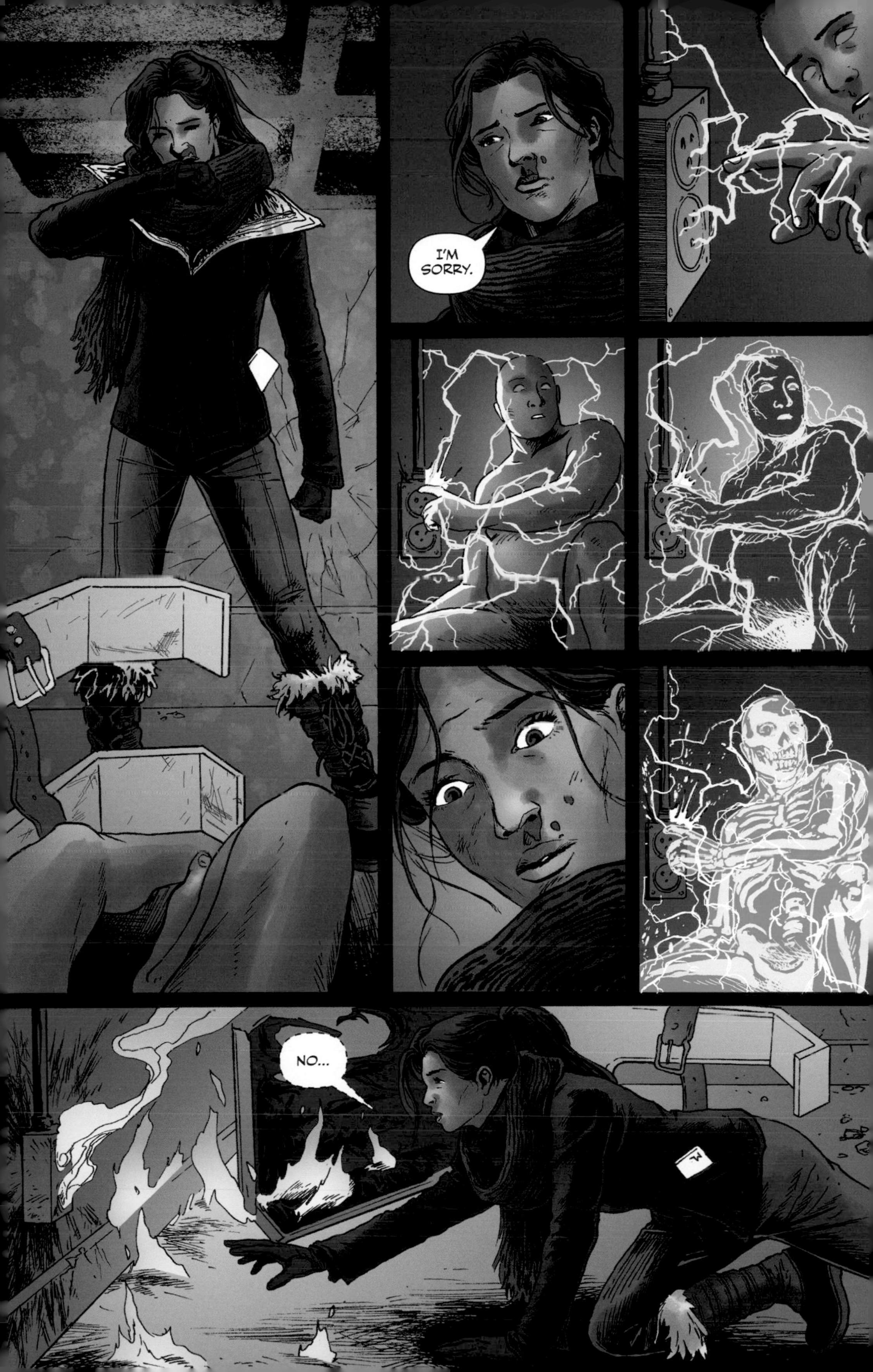
I'M SORRY.
NO...

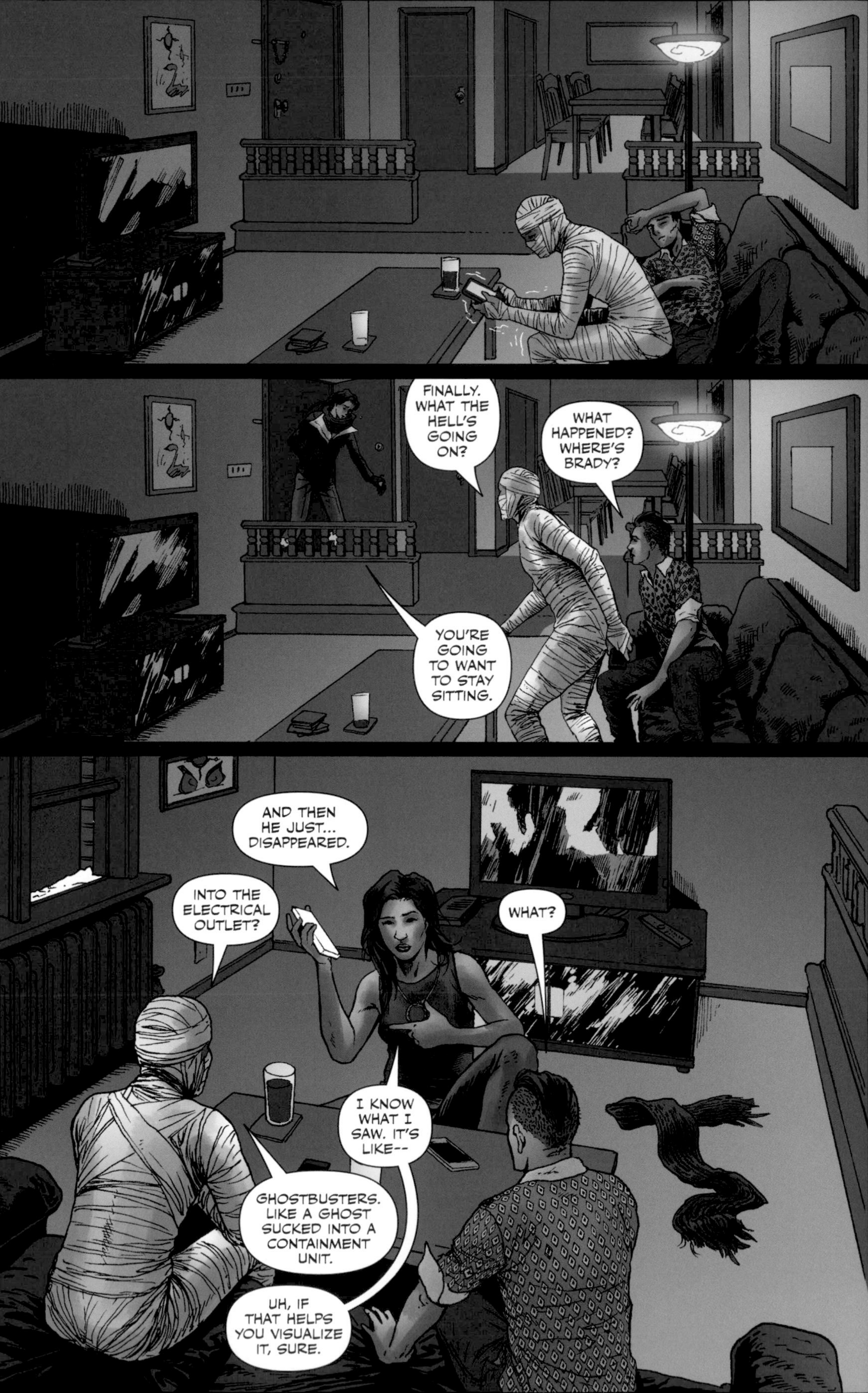
FINALLY. WHAT THE HELL'S GOING ON?
WHAT HAPPENED? WHERE'S BRADY?
YOU'RE GOING TO WANT TO STAY SITTING.
AND THEN HE JUST... DISAPPEARED.
INTO THE ELECTRICAL OUTLET?
WHAT?
I KNOW WHAT I SAW. IT'S LIKE--
GHOSTBUSTERS. LIKE A GHOST SUCKED INTO A CONTAINMENT UNIT.
UH, IF THAT HELPS YOU VISUALIZE IT, SURE.

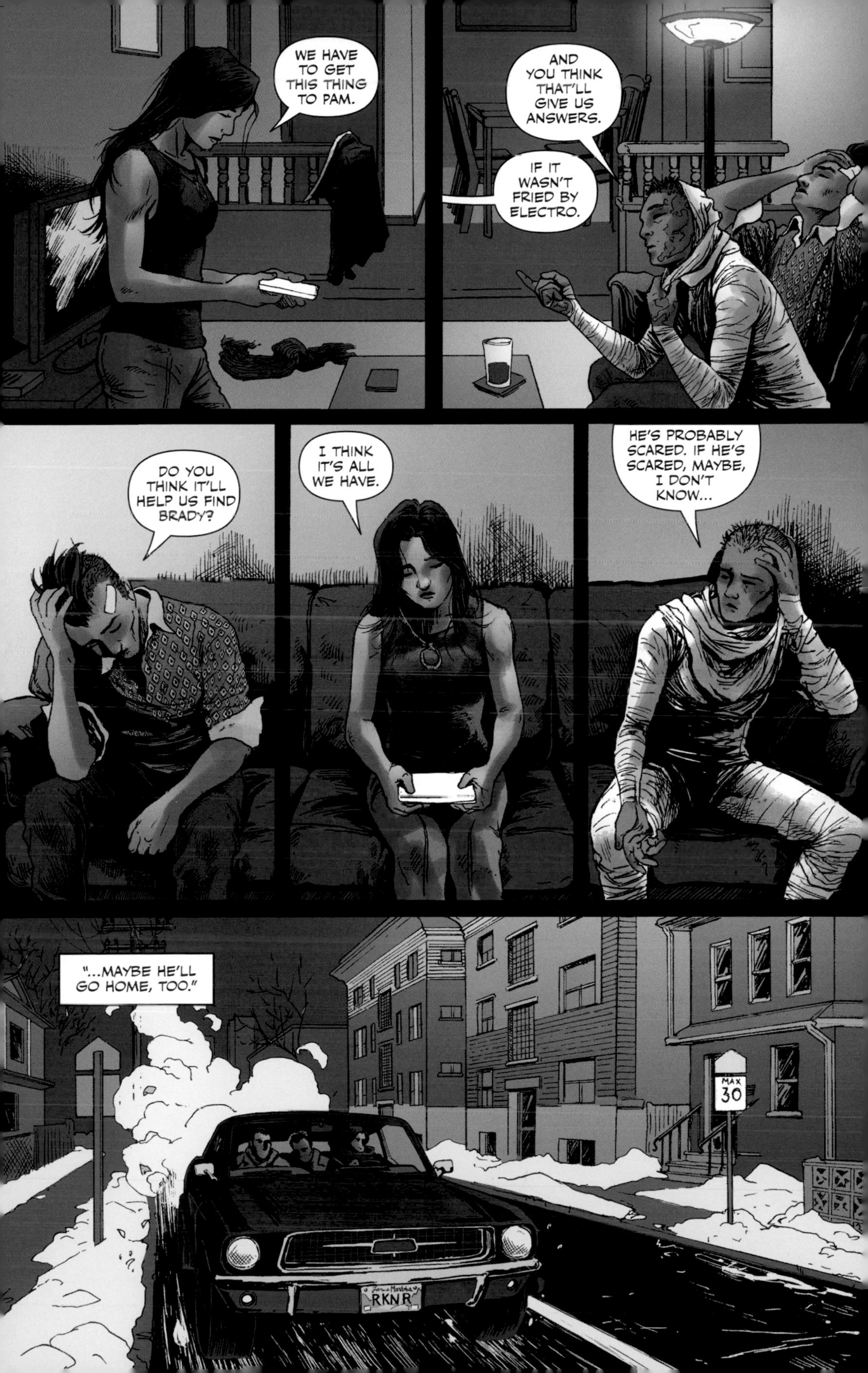
WE HAVE TO GET THIS THING TO PAM.
AND YOU THINK THAT'LL GIVE US ANSWERS.
IF IT WASN'T FRIED BY ELECTRO.
DO YOU THINK IT'LL HELP US FIND BRADY?
I THINK IT'S ALL WE HAVE.
HE'S PROBABLY SCARED. IF HE'S SCARED, MAYBE, I DON'T KNOW...
"...MAYBE HE'LL GO HOME, TOO."
MAX 30
RKNR

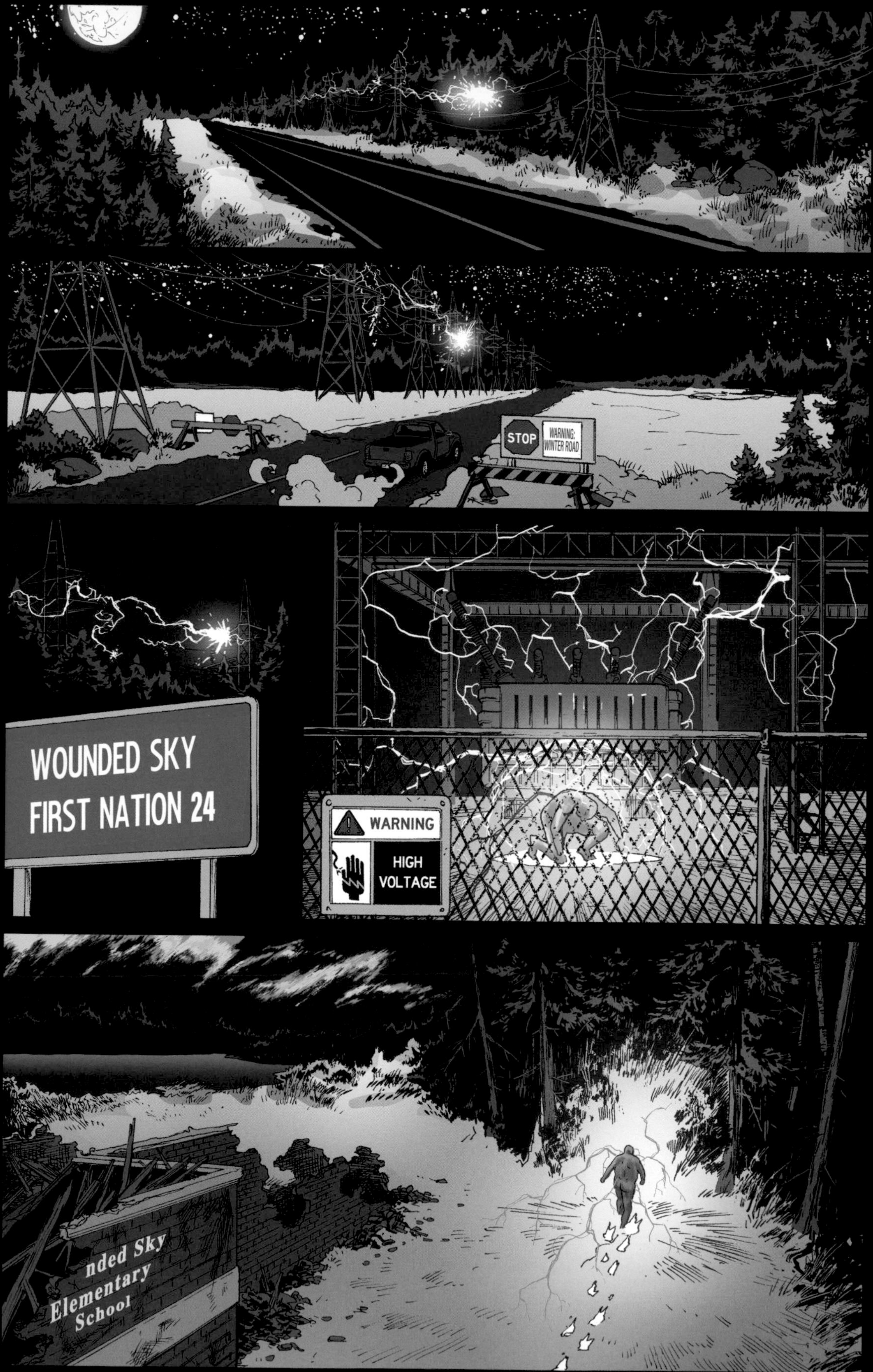
STOP
WARNING: WINTER ROAD
WOUNDED SKY
FIRST NATION 24
WARNING
HIGH VOLTAGE
nded Sky
Elementary
School

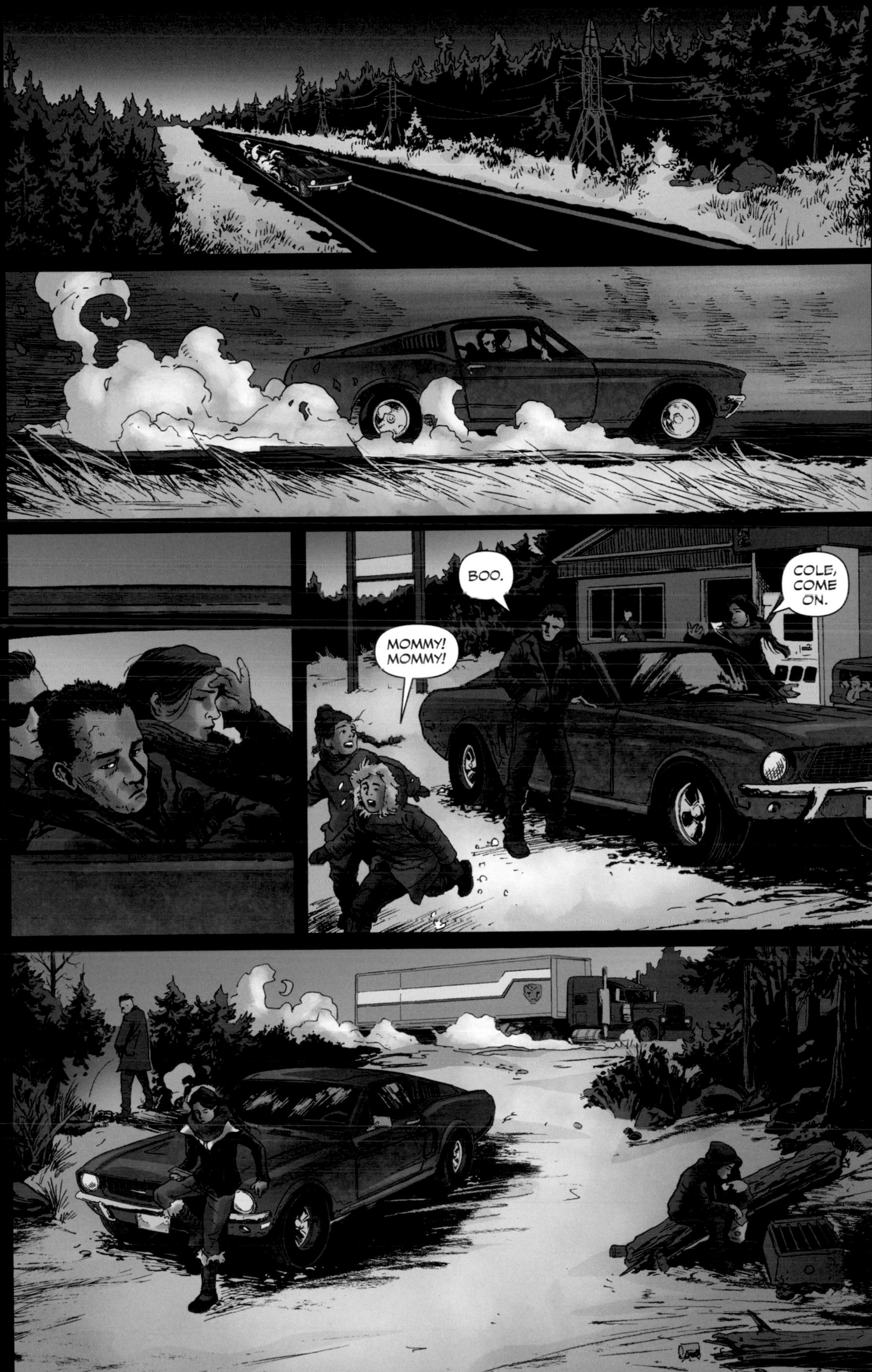
BOO.
COLE, COME ON.
MOMMY! MOMMY!

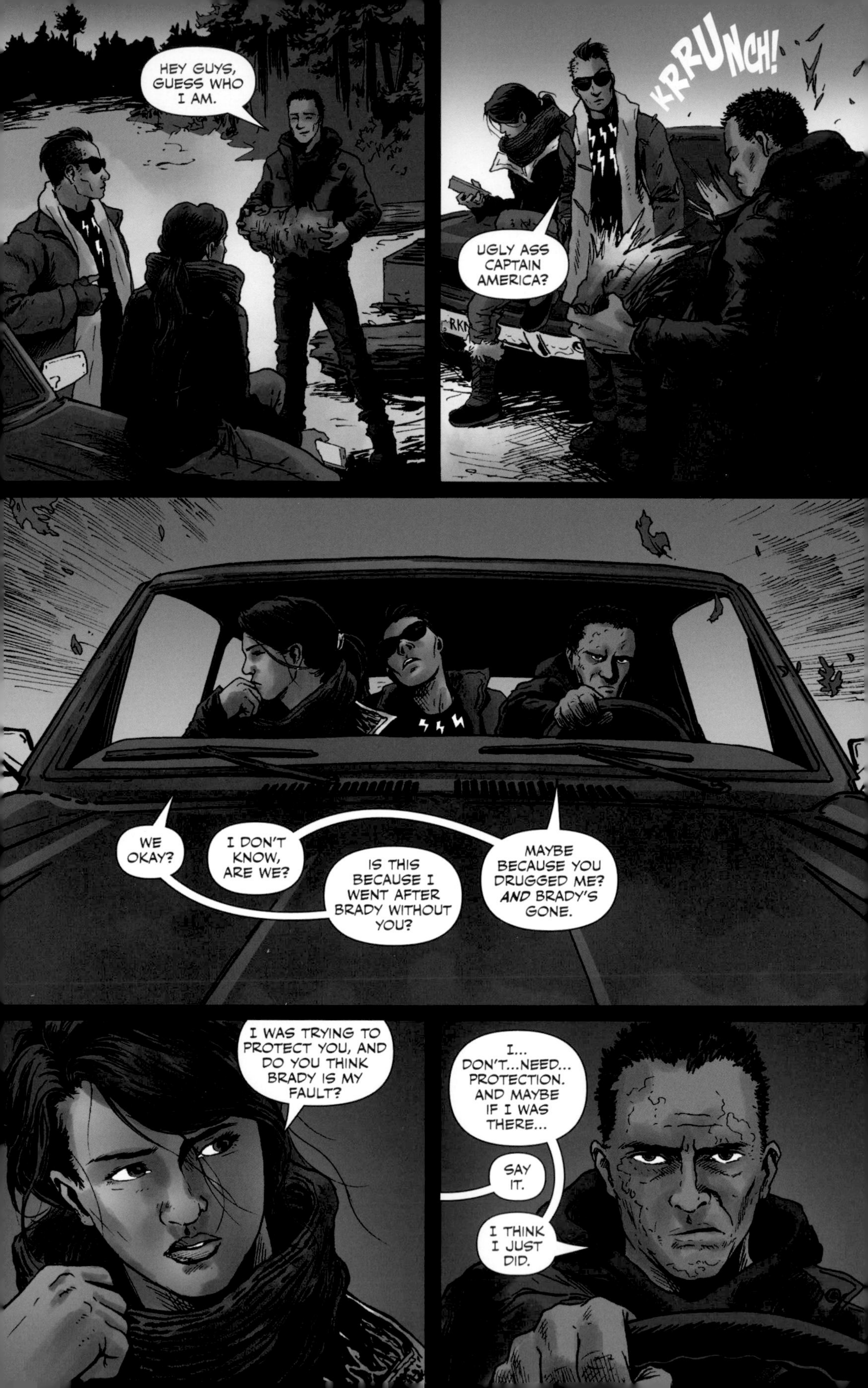
HEY GUYS, GUESS WHO I AM.
KRRUNCH!
UGLY ASS CAPTAIN AMERICA?
WE OKAY?
I DON'T KNOW, ARE WE?
IS THIS BECAUSE I WENT AFTER BRADY WITHOUT YOU?
MAYBE BECAUSE YOU DRUGGED ME? *AND* BRADY'S GONE.
I WAS TRYING TO PROTECT YOU, AND DO YOU THINK BRADY IS MY FAULT?
I... DON'T...NEED... PROTECTION. AND MAYBE IF I WAS THERE...
SAY IT.
I THINK I JUST DID.

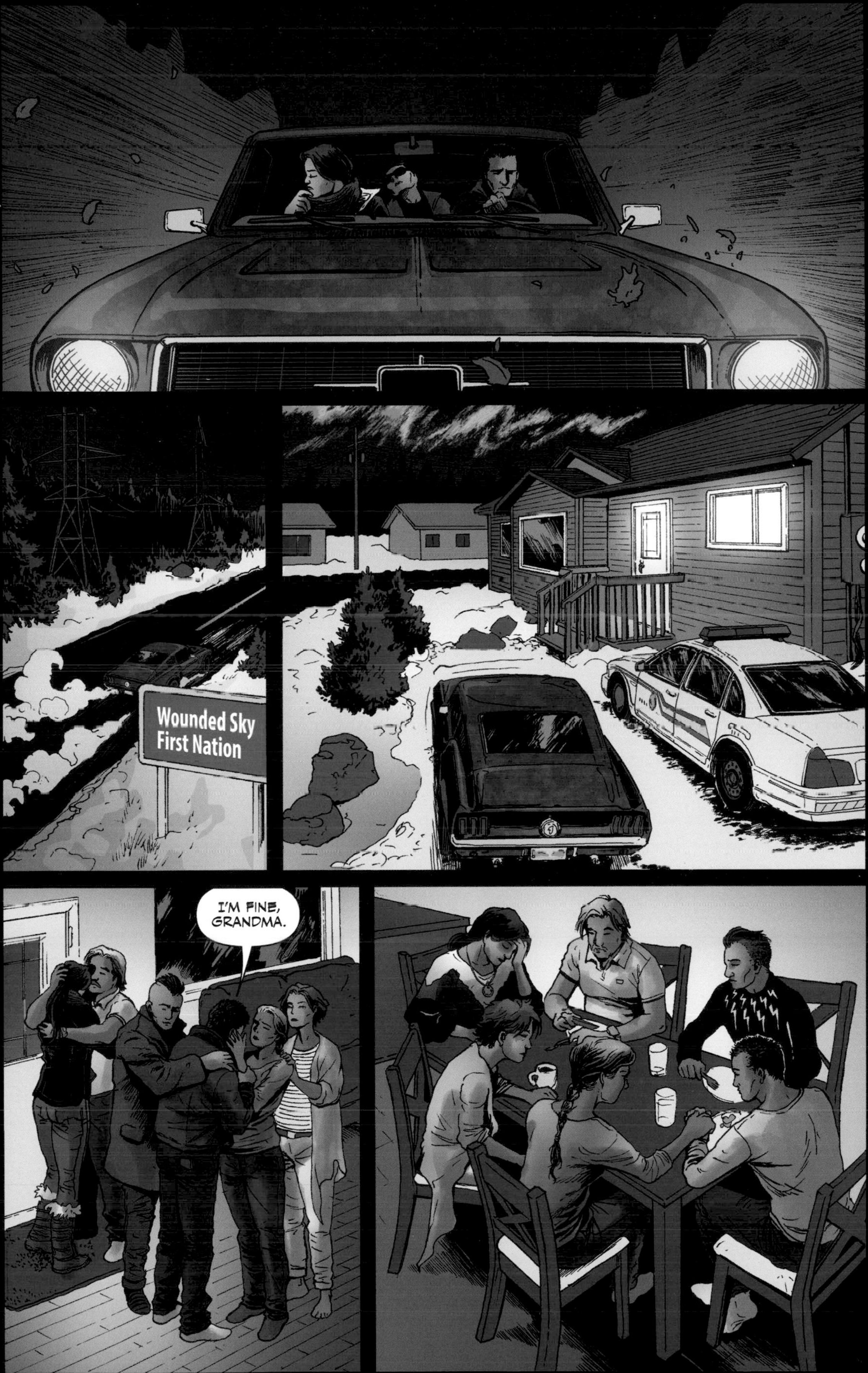
Wounded Sky
First Nation
I'M FINE,
GRANDMA.

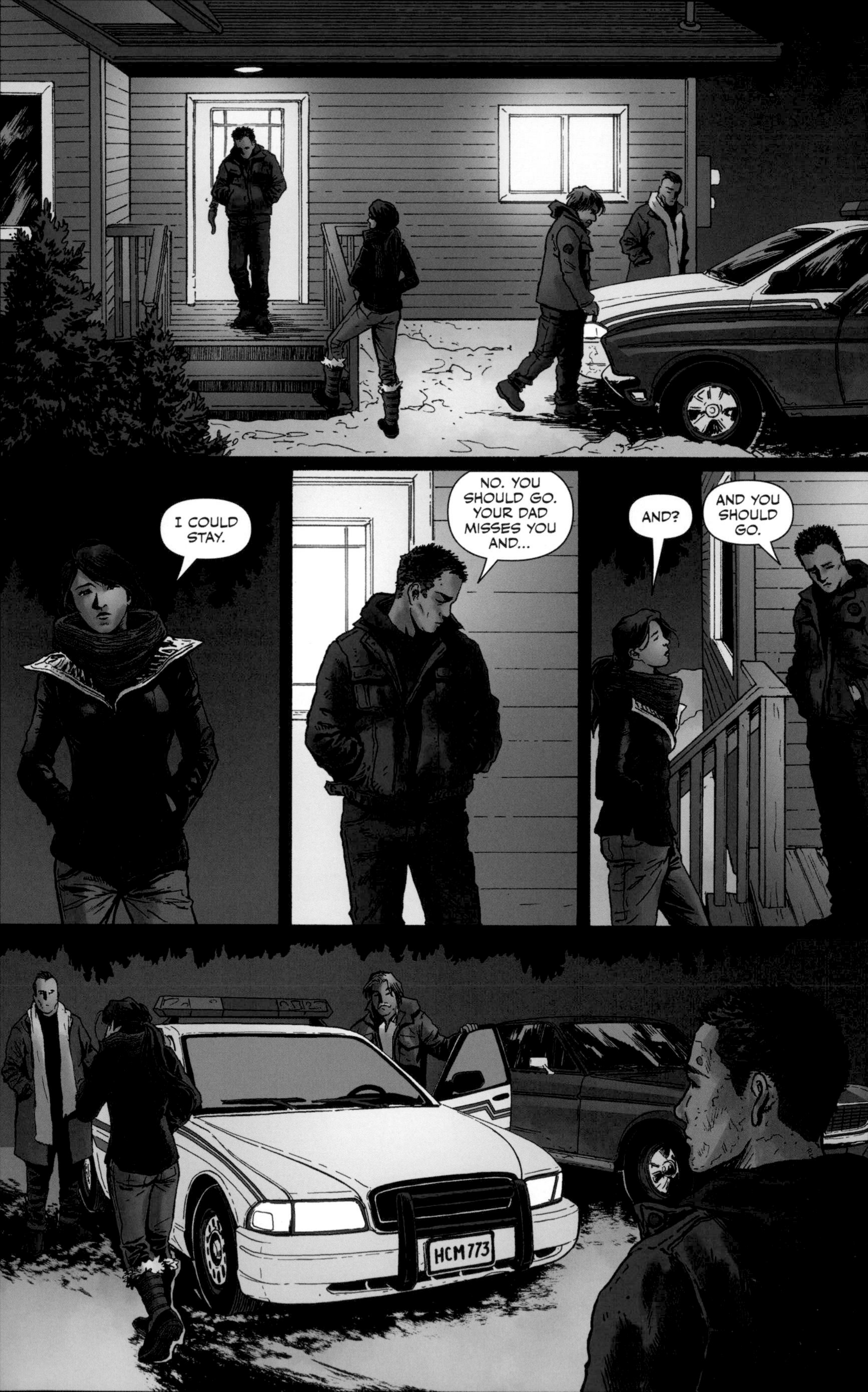
I COULD STAY.
NO. YOU SHOULD GO. YOUR DAD MISSES YOU AND...
AND?
AND YOU SHOULD GO.
HCM 773

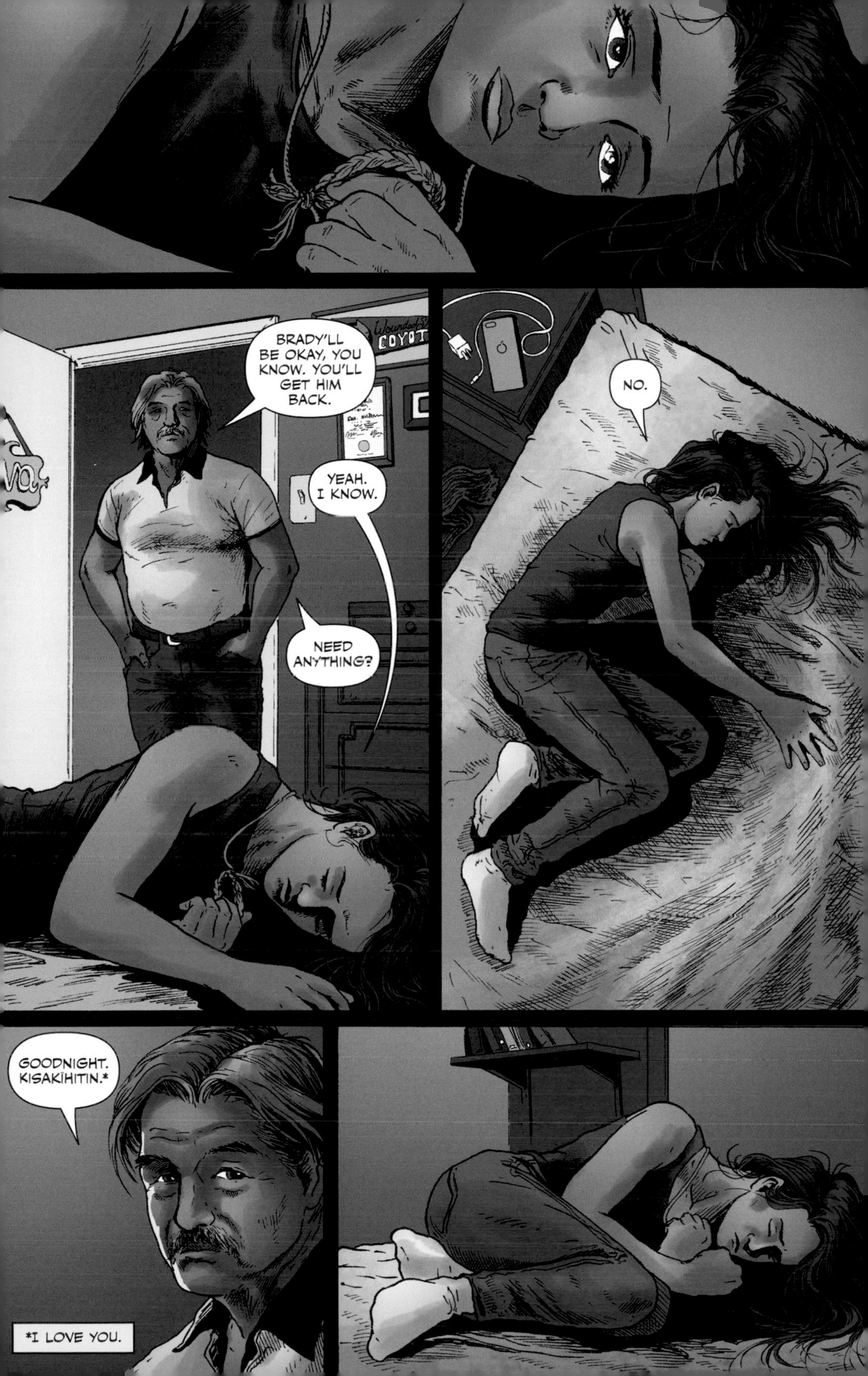
BRADY'LL BE OKAY, YOU KNOW. YOU'LL GET HIM BACK.
YEAH. I KNOW.
NEED ANYTHING?
NO.
GOODNIGHT. KISAKÎHITIN.*
*I LOVE YOU.

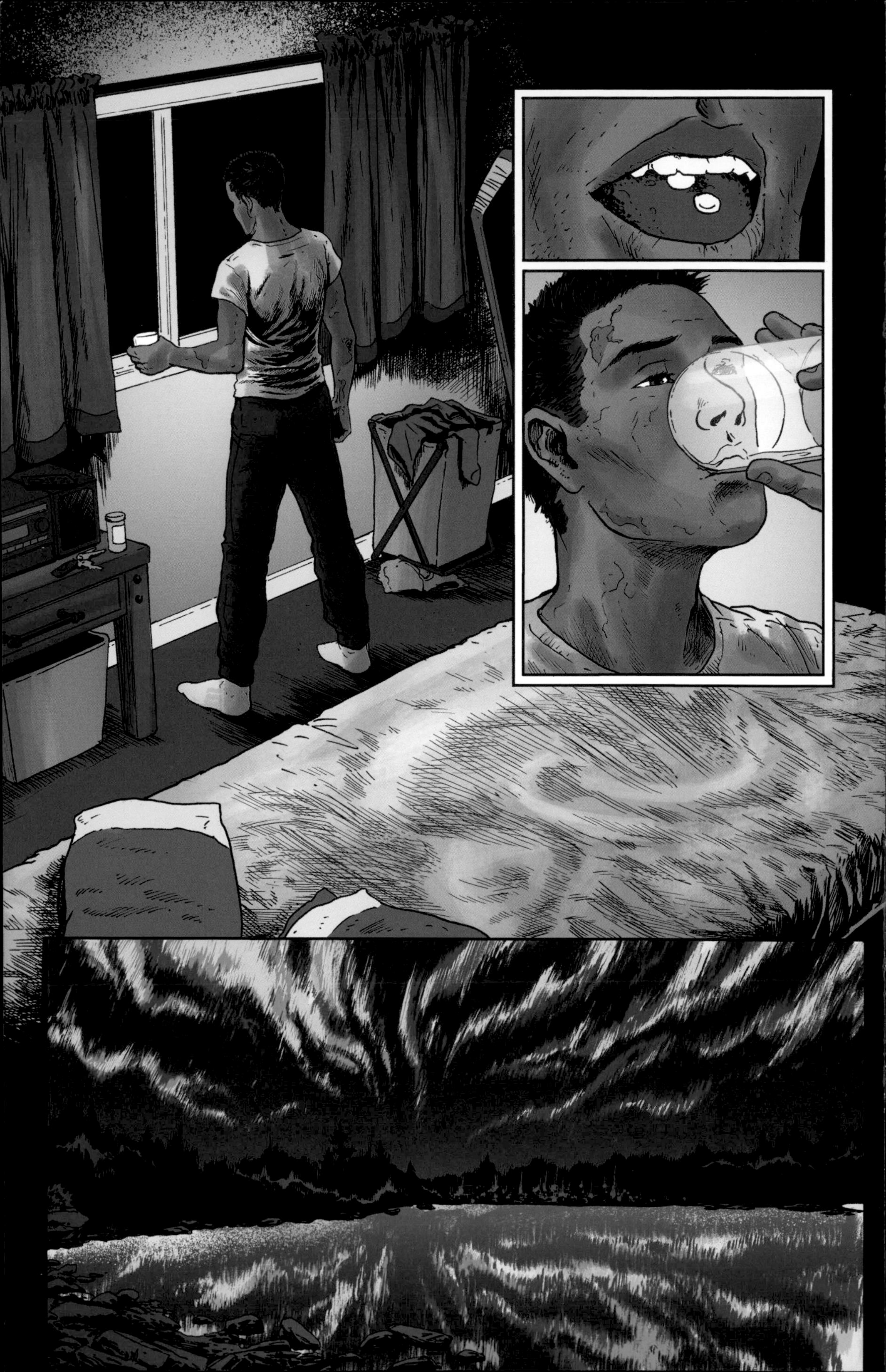

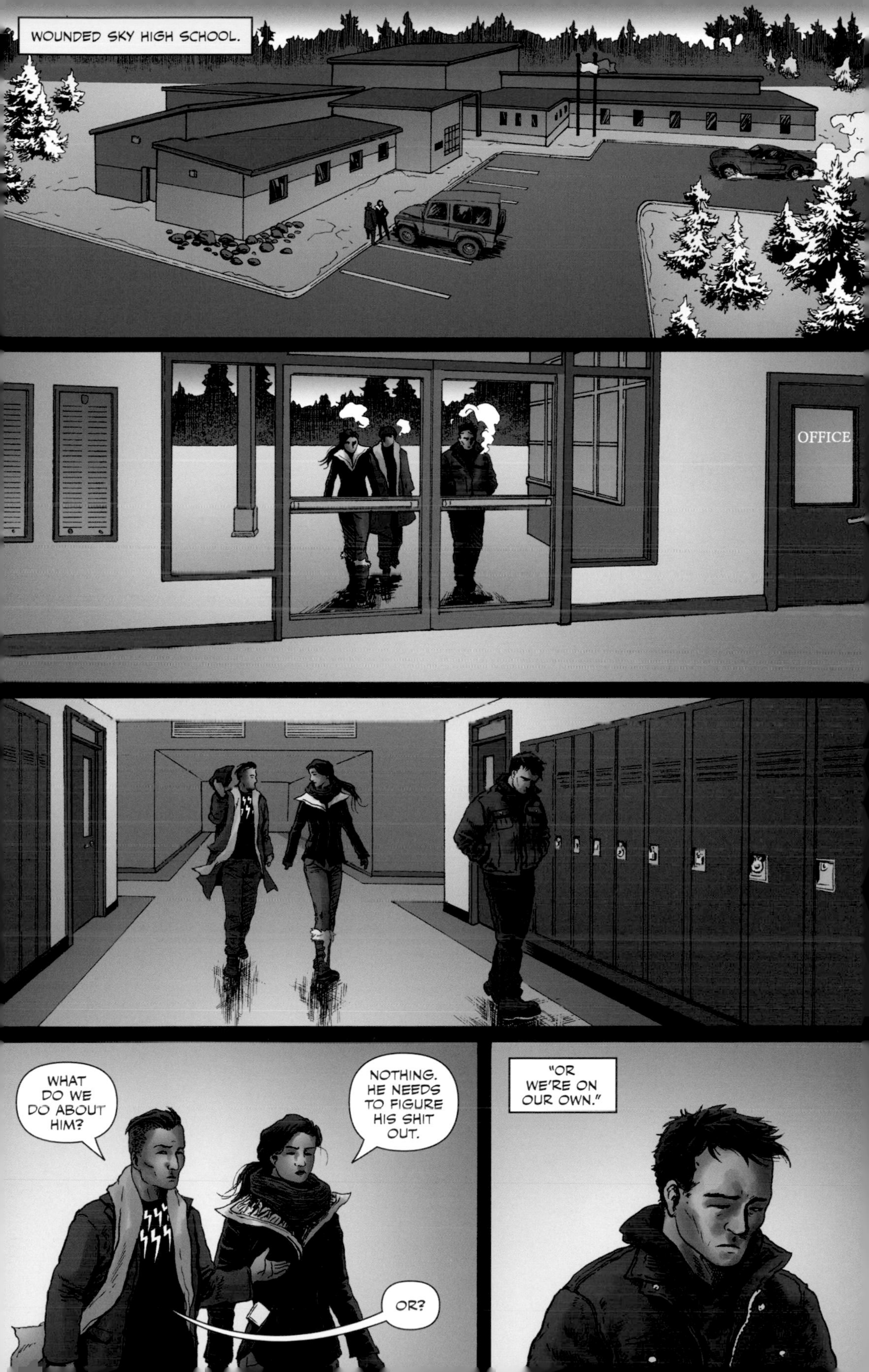
WOUNDED SKY HIGH SCHOOL.
OFFICE
WHAT DO WE DO ABOUT HIM?
NOTHING. HE NEEDS TO FIGURE HIS SHIT OUT.
OR?
"OR WE'RE ON OUR OWN."

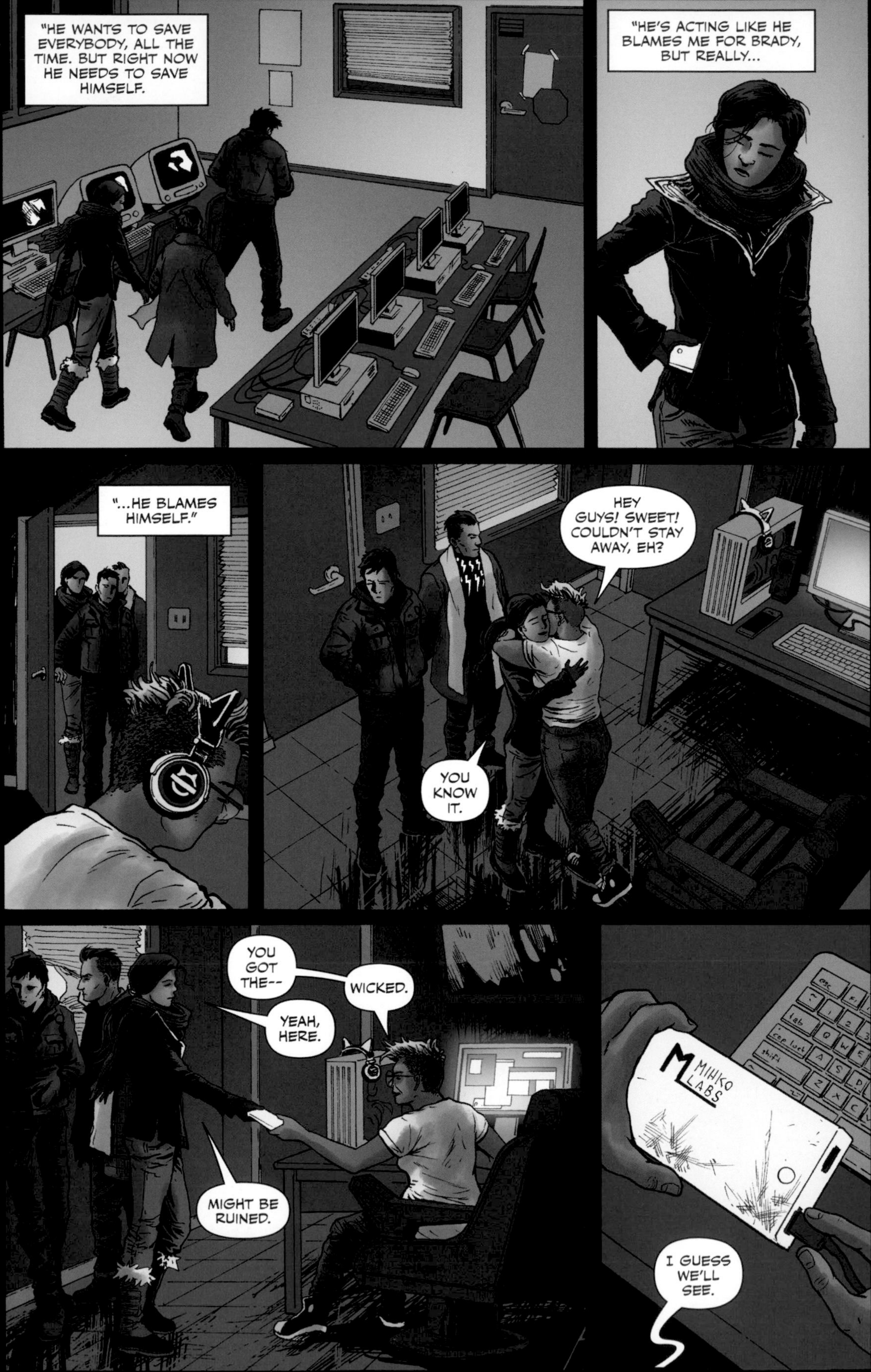
"HE WANTS TO SAVE EVERYBODY, ALL THE TIME. BUT RIGHT NOW HE NEEDS TO SAVE HIMSELF.
"HE'S ACTING LIKE HE BLAMES ME FOR BRADY, BUT REALLY...
"...HE BLAMES HIMSELF."
HEY GUYS! SWEET! COULDN'T STAY AWAY, EH?
YOU KNOW IT.
YOU GOT THE--
WICKED.
YEAH, HERE.
MIGHT BE RUINED.
MIHKO LABS
I GUESS WE'LL SEE.

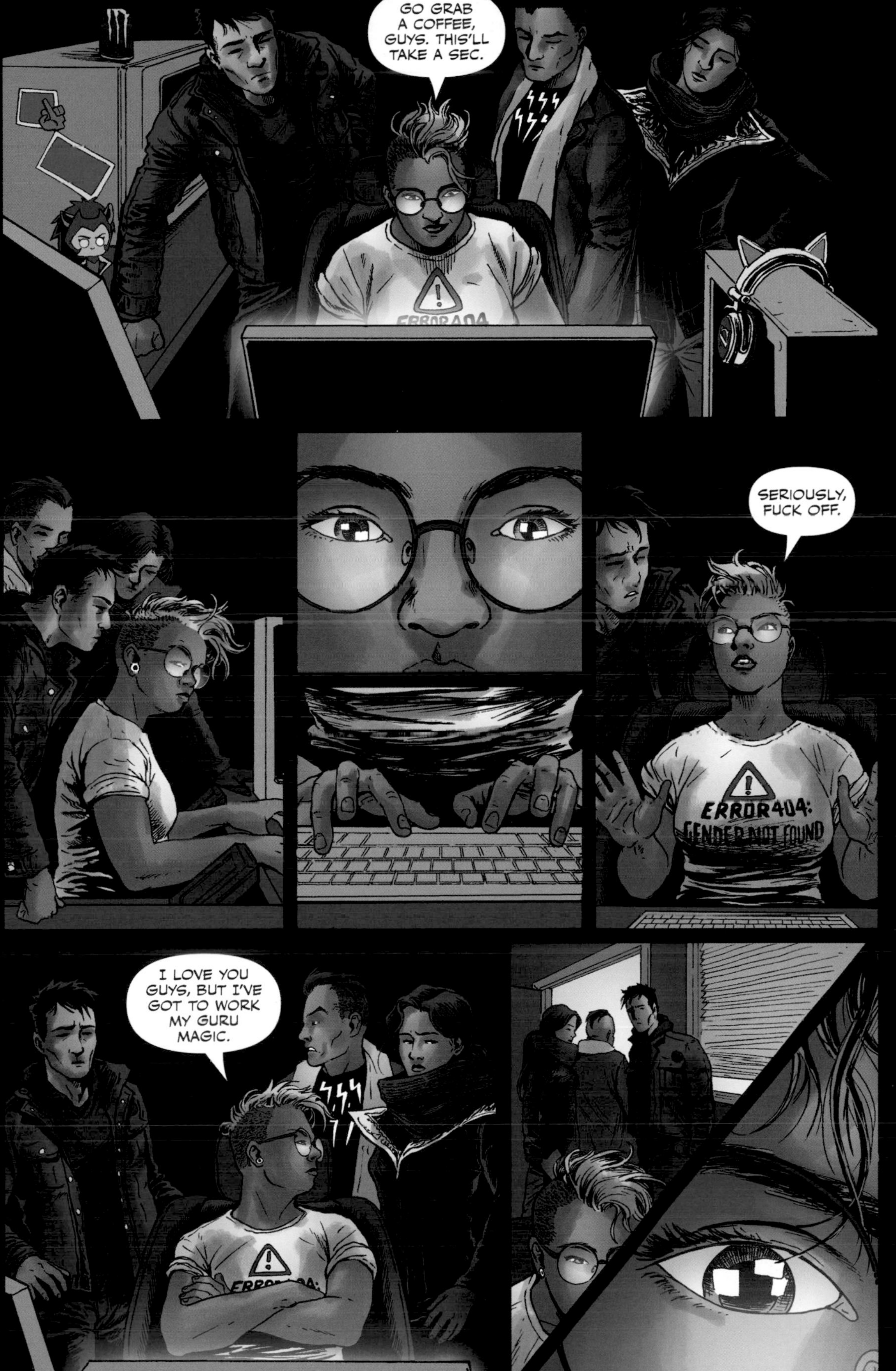
GO GRAB A COFFEE, GUYS. THIS'LL TAKE A SEC.
SERIOUSLY, FUCK OFF.
ERROR404: GENDER NOT FOUND
I LOVE YOU GUYS, BUT I'VE GOT TO WORK MY GURU MAGIC.

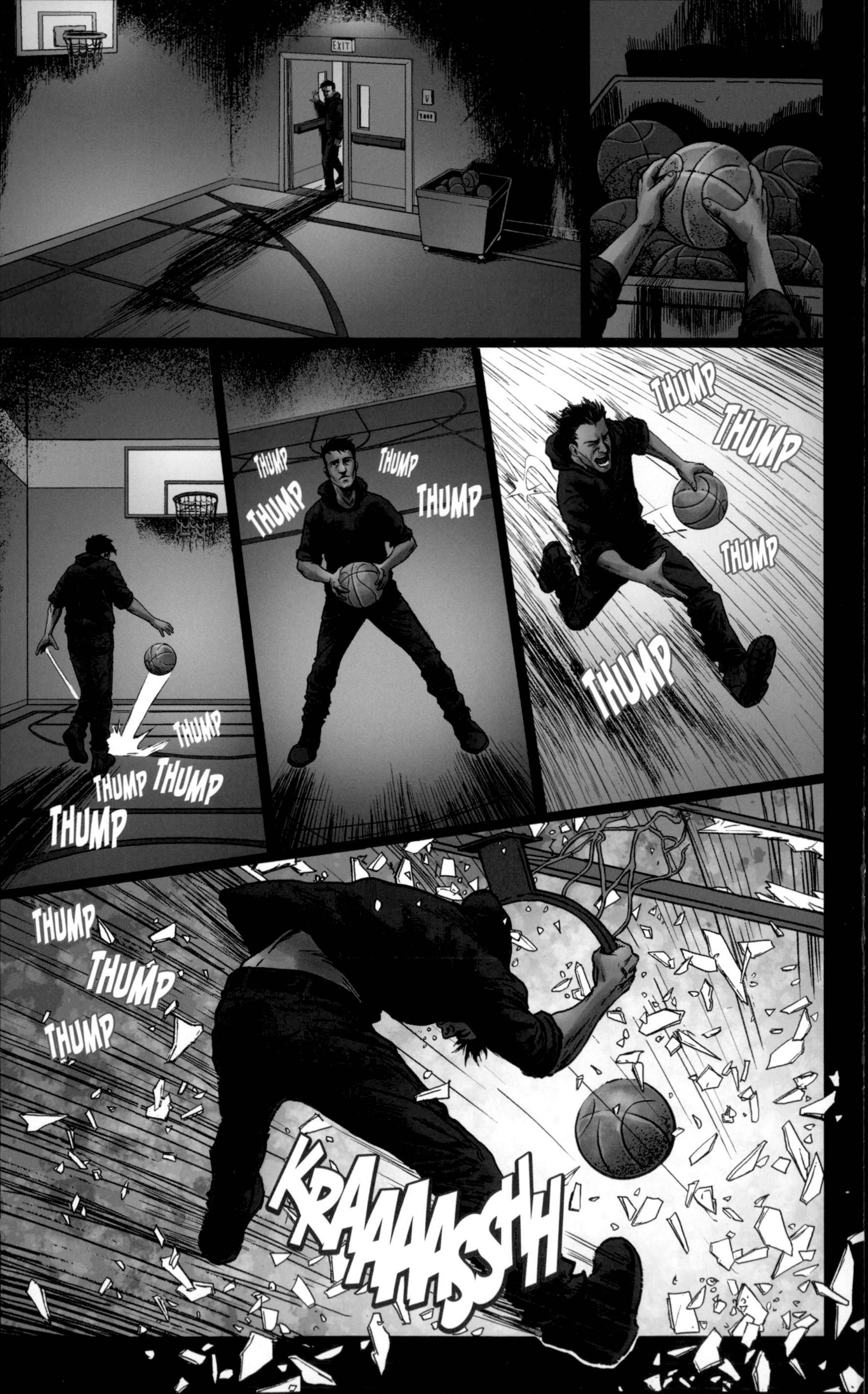
EXIT
THUMP
THUMP
THUMP
THUMP
THUMP
THUMP
THUMP
THUMP
THUMP
THUMP
THUMP
THUMP
THUMP
THUMP
THUMP
KRAAAASHH

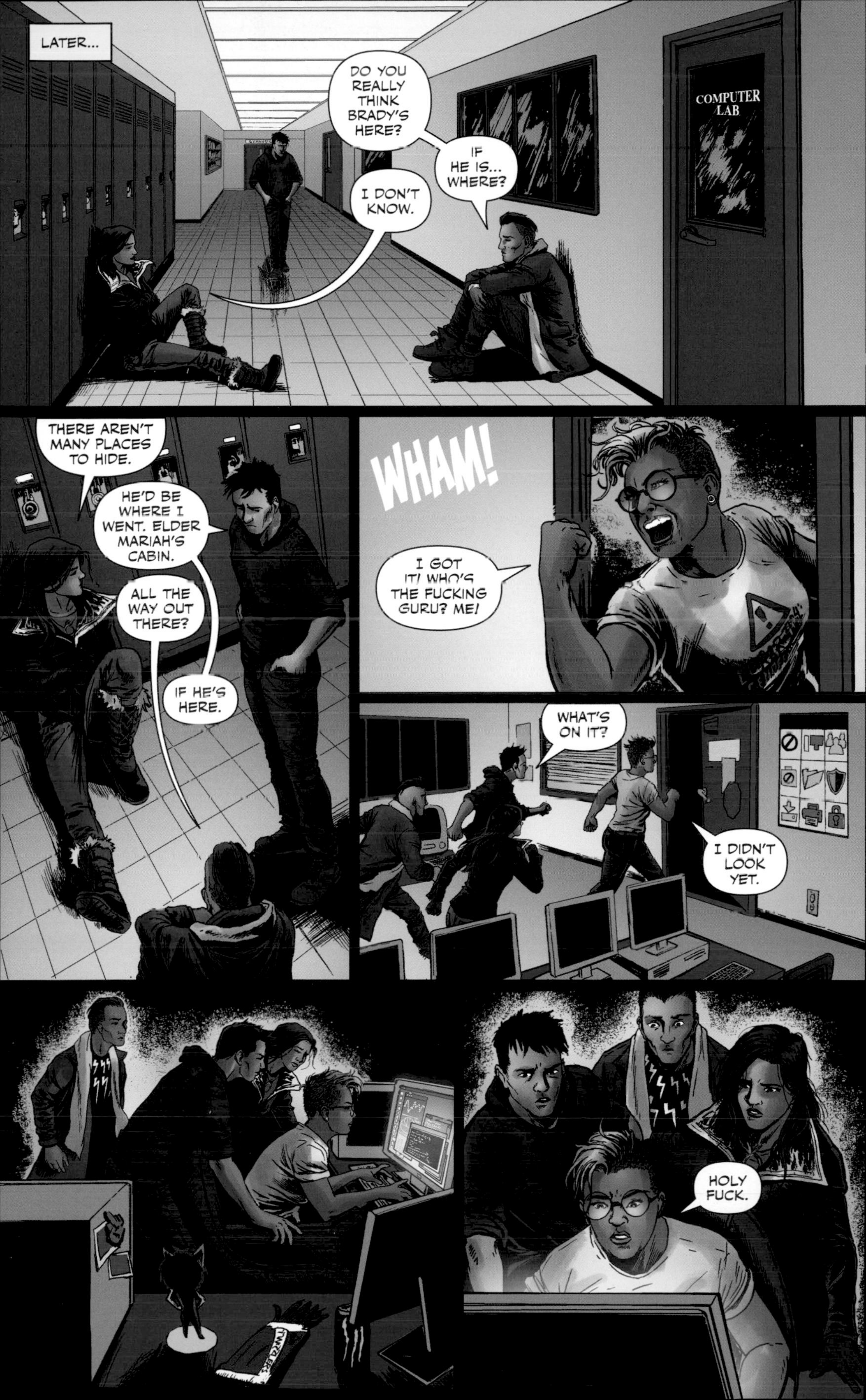
LATER...
COMPUTER LAB
DO YOU REALLY THINK BRADY'S HERE?
IF HE IS... WHERE?
I DON'T KNOW.
THERE AREN'T MANY PLACES TO HIDE.
HE'D BE WHERE I WENT. ELDER MARIAH'S CABIN.
ALL THE WAY OUT THERE?
IF HE'S HERE.
WHAM!
I GOT IT! WHO'S THE FUCKING GURU? ME!
WHAT'S ON IT?
I DIDN'T LOOK YET.
HOLY FUCK.

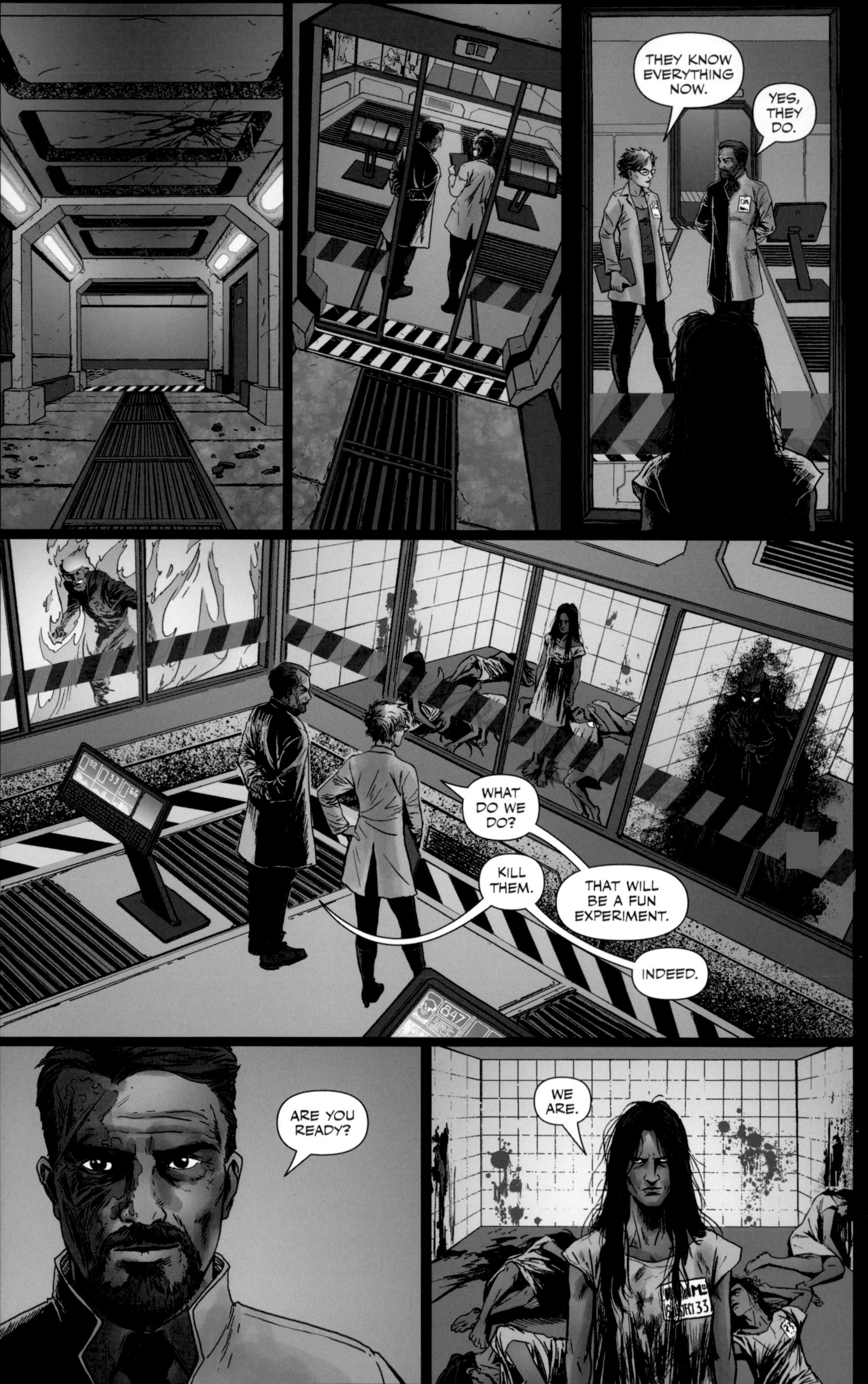
THEY KNOW EVERYTHING NOW.
YES, THEY DO.
WHAT DO WE DO?
KILL THEM.
THAT WILL BE A FUN EXPERIMENT.
INDEED.
ARE YOU READY?
WE ARE.

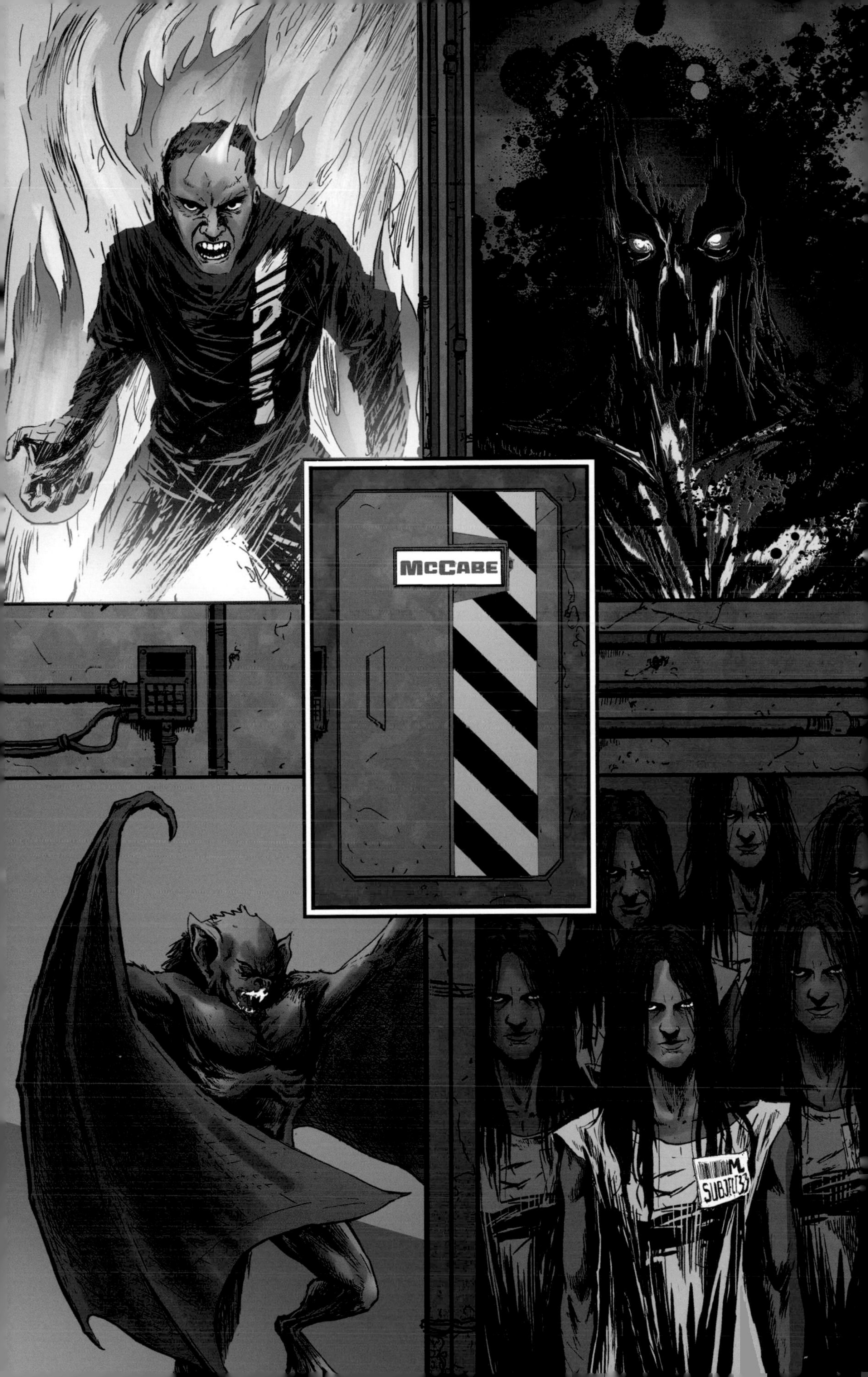
McCABE
M.
SUBJECT 33

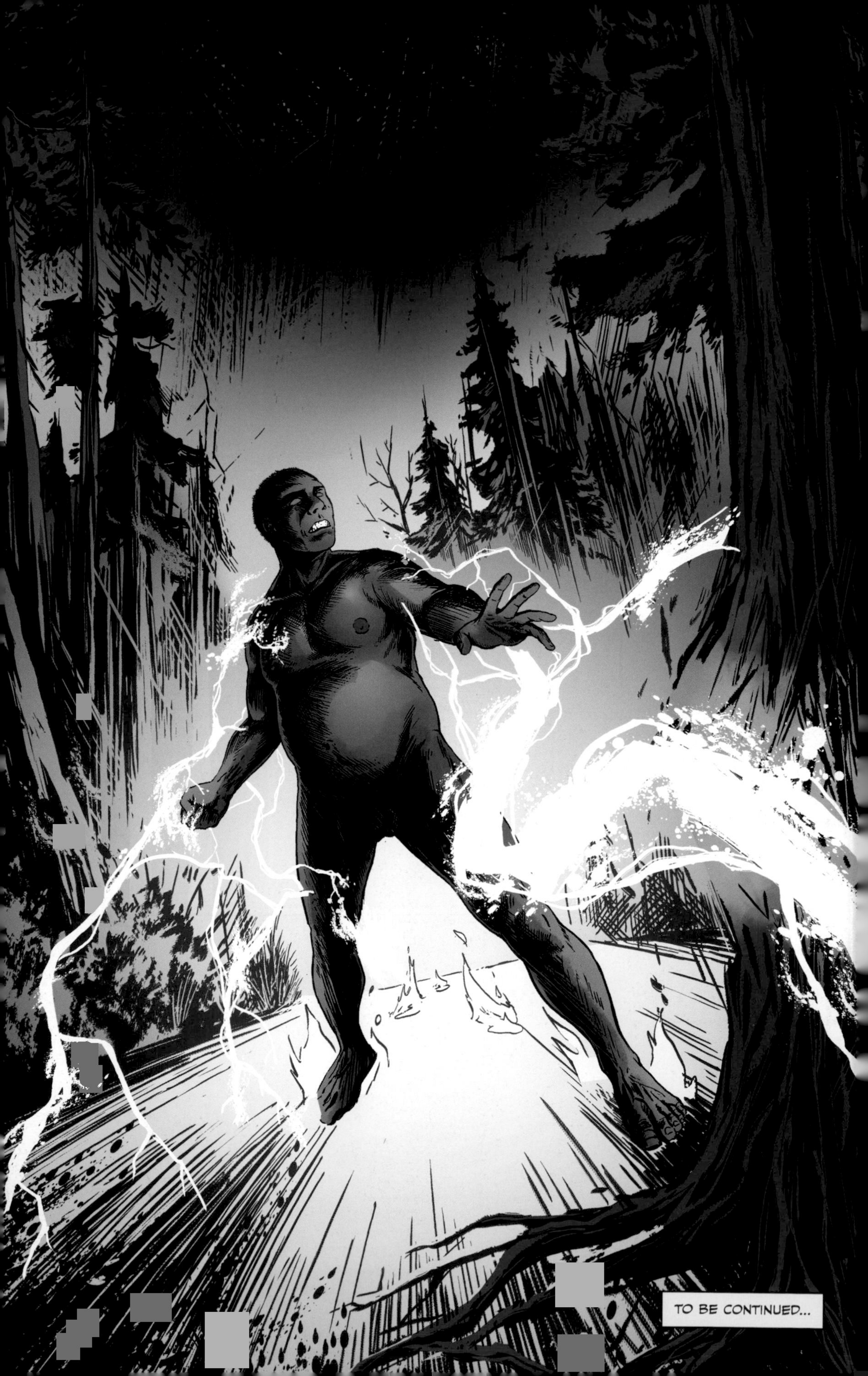
TO BE CONTINUED...

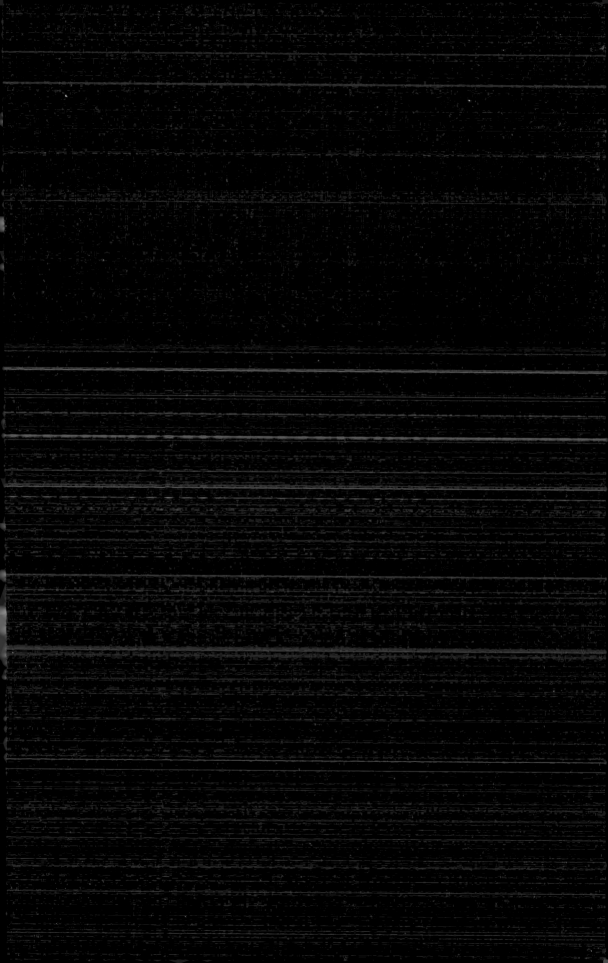

DAVID A. ROBERTSON (he, him, his) is the 2021 recipient of the Writer's Union of Canada's Freedom to Read Award. He is the author of more than 25 books for young readers including *When We Were Alone*, which won a Governor General's Literary Award and was a finalist for the TD Canadian Children's Literature Award. David's recent works include the graphic novel *Breakdown* (The Reckoner Rises, Vol. 1), middle grade novel *The Barren Grounds*, children's book *On the Trapline*, and memoir *Black Water: Family, Legacy, and Blood Memory*. He is also the writer and host of the podcast *Kíwew*, which won the 2021 RTDNA Prairie Region Award for Best Podcast. A sought-after speaker and educator, David is a member of Norway House Cree Nation. He lives in Winnipeg. | @DaveAlexRoberts

SCOTT B. HENDERSON (he, him, his) is author/illustrator of the sci-fi/fantasy comic, *The Chronicles of Era*. Scott has illustrated The Reckoner Rises series; A Girl Called Echo series; and *7 Generations*; select titles in the Tales From Big Spirit series; select stories in *This Place: 150 Years Retold*; *Fire Starters* (an AIYLA Honour Book); and the Eisner-award nominee, *A Blanket of Butterflies*. In 2016, he was the recipient of the C4 Central Canada Comic Con Storyteller Award. Find Scott on social media @Ouroboros09

Since 1998, colourist **DONOVAN YACIUK** (he, him, his) has worked on books published by Marvel, DC, Dark Horse comics, and HighWater Press, including the A Girl Called Echo series and *This Place: 150 Years Retold*. Donovan holds a Bachelor of Fine Arts (Honours) from the University of Manitoba and began his career as a part of the legendary Digital Chameleon colouring studio. He lives in Winnipeg, Manitoba, Canada. | @yaciuk

ANDREW THOMAS (he, him, his) is an award-winning artist and letterer from Southwestern Ontario who has worked with Disney, Archie, and even Silent Bob himself—Kevin Smith. He's the co-creator and artist of the award-winning Canadian comic series, Auric of the Great White North. He has illustrated covers and interiors for books such as *Archie's Friend Scarlet*, *Captain Canuck*, *Canuck Adventures*, and more. In addition to illustration, Andrew is also an accomplished letterer with over 100 published comics to his name. Follow him on Instagram @thefatmanwholetters

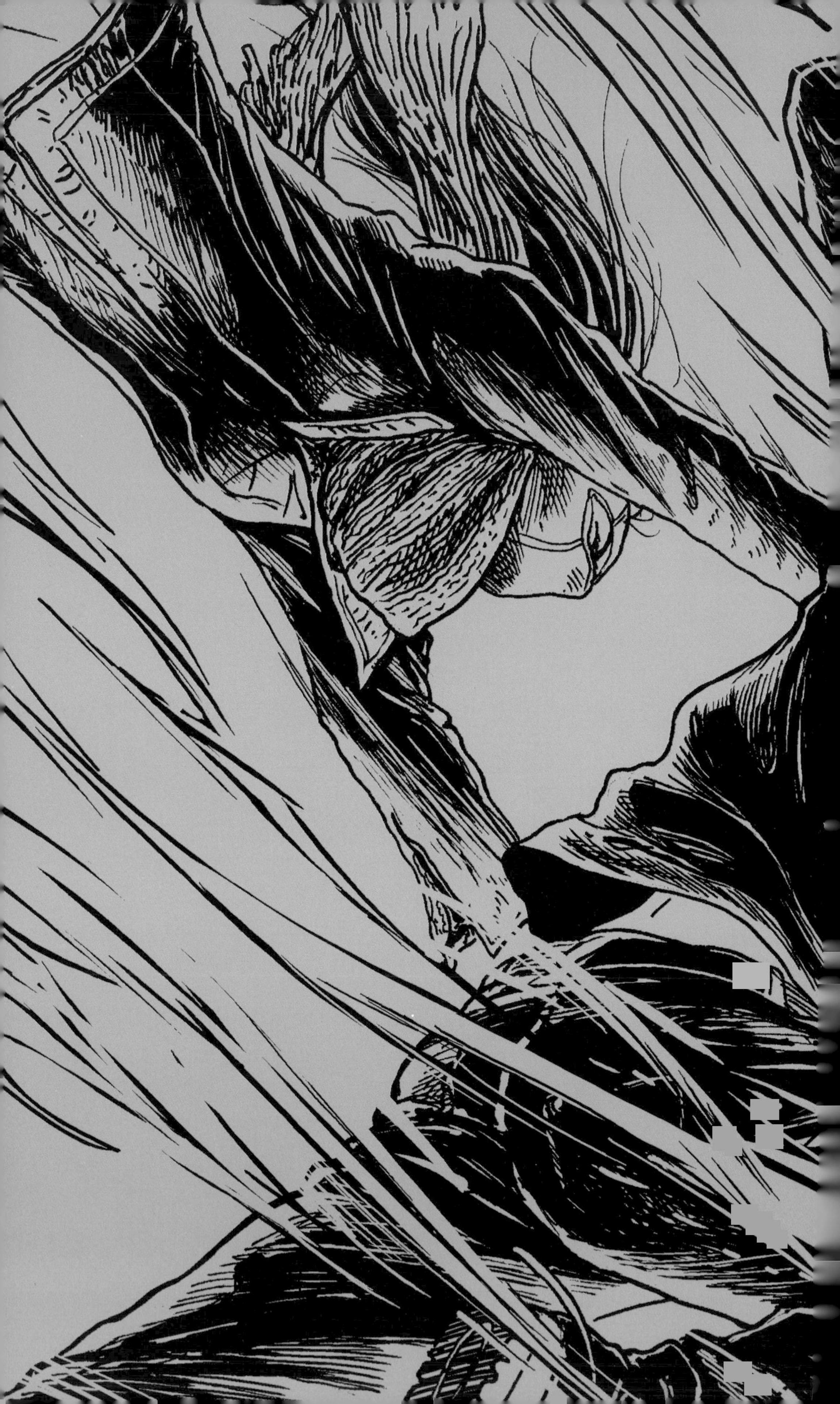